A.J. Dailey

'FORE'-Warned

'FORE'-Warned

ISBN: 9781638926337

Printed in the United States of AmericaThis book is printed on acid-free paper

Table of Contents

Book I

Book II

Book III

'FORE'-Warned

Book I

CHAPTER ONE

The reporter was on his way to a meeting he hoped would leadhim to solve a mystery that had hit the golf world almost twentyyears ago. During this time, he never turned up a clue about the disappearance of Jack Proctor. Out of the blue, he received a phone callsetting up this face-to-face meeting arranged by the long-lost golfer.

The man vanished without a trace, two days after winning the British Open, the world's most prestigious golf tournament. Severalmonths earlier, He had won the U. S. Open. He was an unknown amateur, coming out of the blue to shock everyone with outstandinggolf skills.

The twenty-year-old had never played a round away from the country club he belonged to. He was regarded as a good player by his fellow members, but no one said they ever saw him perform as he did in being one of the youngest amateurs to ever win these majorgolf events. The shock turned to amazement when the man disappeared right after winning two prestigious golf tournaments.

Jim Carraige was a cub reporter, covering the American contest, this fateful year. His efforts were completely directed toward the big-name professionals. No one had paid any attention to the young golfer, except one article that mentioned him briefly. The reporter quoted one of the players whosaid he saw a man, whom he did not know, displaying a 'nice' swing.Jack was identified as the golfer. Except for this minor detail, no one appeared to have noticed him before he began his first round.

CHAPTER TWO

Everything quickly changed when Jack finished his roundwithout a bogie and one birdie. His one-under score put him in third place, only a couple of shots from the leader. This was most remarkable since none of the other players came within two shots ofpar. Suddenly, Jack Proctor was in the spotlight, so to speak. But itdid not fluster the young golfer. He dodged all questions about himselfpersonally, stating he would not talk about anything other than this golf match and only after the tournament was over.

A reporter wrote: 'I began researching Jack's play in the qualifying rounds after he shot himself into a tie for first place at the end of the second round. No one saw anything spectacular in his game or his scores. He had played just well enough to get himself a slot in the 'Open', he said. 'I did not find out a whole lot about the man. The members of his club refrained from discussing him, noting that he valued his privacy. They mentioned only that he had experienced a very tragic event in his life and had requested them not to disclose his circumstances, he wrote.

Now, Jack was leading, going into the final round, and the day began with a buzz. He had declined to be interviewed after eachof the first three days, stating he would not talk to anyone untilthe tournament was over. He had again refused to be interviewed and moved to the first tee immediately, without warming up on the driving range or the putting greens.

The final round was a sweet thing to watch if you were a fan of Jack Proctor, and he had gained a huge host of followers. His play wasalmost flawless. Not brilliant, just steady and good enough to win--going away.

His interview after the tournament was short. He declined to discuss his life, thanked everyone, and disappeared.

CHAPTER THREE

Jim wrote his story and turned it over to his editor. 'I went to thefarm where Jack lives, but it was closed. The two families who had lived there for years, working with his father, were gone. None of his neighbors could offer any clues as to his whereabouts, he said.

'I want you to stay on this full-time. This is a big event. For the guy to win the Open is huge, and then I just got word that he hasentered to play in the British Open. By winning our Open, he qualifies to play over there. I can't imagine why he has gone underground like this, so to speak. Let's go all out on finding this fellow,' the editor said.

The reporter felt he would locate Jack Proctor when he traveled to England, so he checked every possible way he could get there. Jackwas not booked to travel to England by commercial means, airliners,private carriers, or ships. He contacted all the charter firms, but no Jack. 'Either someone is not telling me the truth, or the guy is going byrowboat', Jim told his editor.

'Well, get over there and cover the tournament. He will turn up there, for sure. I'm sending a camera crew with you for full coverage,' the editor said.

The week of the sports event arrived, and still no Jack. The practice rounds had begun for all the other players, and it was soon the opening day of the tournament. Two hours before the first tee time,a car pulled up to the player's entrance and out stepped the missingAmerican player and his caddie. He was dressed to play golf, downto his shoes, and the two proceeded to the starting area without talking to anyone outside the perimeter. The reporter, Jim Carraige,was not allowed to bring his camera crew, so he walked alone withthe American group. As he approached, he was told to produce hisidentification papers. And was given a thorough examination. Jim noticed that every reporter went through the same routine. This wasunheard of at the British Open, and it only happened around Jack Proctor's two-some.

'Something was going on, for sure. Maybe this explains the odd behavior of the American open winner. He seems to be under somesort of protection,' Jim thought.

CHAPTER FOUR

The golfers teed off and were followed by a bunch of security people, while ahead and to the sides were other men movingalong with them. Jim noticed only a few cameras in view. Usually, there would be at least a hundred in the crowd of reporters followingthis high-powered pair of golfers. Something is up, he thought again.But there were no instances, and Jack fired a four-under par round, good for a first-place lead.

Instead of meeting with the media, the group of men who walked the entire round herded the golfer and his caddie to a waiting car and leftwith escort cars and motorbikes. The officials immediately assembled the media in a closed area.

'There has been a death threat directed at Jack Proctor, and it is the reason for everything unusual happening today. I cannot tell you any more right now. Tomorrow will be like today, and only if the man makes the cut. The FBI and Scotland Yard are here in force. Everything is being done to ensure the safety of this tournament.We are going ahead with the play as advised by the authorities. The only change tomorrow will be an extra space open around Jack's group, and he will be playing alone.

Jack was off early and finished his round two-under, leaving himat six-under and still ahead. No incidents occurred, and he left immediately. The media people were really upset and vented on the officials. 'What kind of threat is keeping us from doing our jobs and talking to the leader?' one American television crew asked. They got the same answer as before.

'We will let you know as soon as we hear anything. We are almost as much in the dark as you are,' the spokesperson said.

The third round began with Jack in the last group. The officials announced there would be a two-some, as the second-place golfer demanded to play with the leader. 'I want him to see me, and I want to look him in the eyes', he said.

It was evident that tensions were higher today. Five people were escorted away before the play began. Two were young females who made quite a scene. This really started the rumors flying. The crowds did nothave to be told to stay back. No one wanted to be very close, but theplay of the young American champion was compelling and brilliant. He shot three-under and had a seven-stroke advantage at the end ofthe day.

CHAPTER FIVE

As the final round commenced, a rumor circulated among the spectators suggesting that attempts might be made to impede Jack from completing the event. Someone did not want him to win this tournament. An even wider space separated the lone golfer. His partner for the third round lost his standing, and no one else demanded to replace him, much to the comfort of the authorities. Jack never acknowledged the throng gathered around him, albeit from a distance. He calmly played flawless golf and won the British Open tournament.

Jack waved to the crowd as he was led to the convoy awaiting him. They packed up and sped off into oblivion. He left the playing fieldand has not been seen or heard from since.

CHAPTER SIX

Now, twenty years later, the cub reporter who had never stopped looking for the young man hoped that the mystery would soonbe solved. Every year, at the start of the American and British tournaments, he wrote about those events. While other reporters mentioned the guy occasionally, he was relentless in his quest for JackProctor. He wanted an answer to this puzzle.

Jim reached his destination. It was an RV overnight park. He drove to the unit described to him and pulled in front. The door opened, and he was invited to enter.

And there the man stood. Jack was surprised how little he had changed. Lean, tanned, with a full head of hair, and showing the easy poise of a man in complete control of his life and his surroundings.They shook hands, and Jack began telling his story:

'I am the only child of Bill and Sally Proctor. We lived on a farm,and until I was one year away from entering college, everything was normal and good in our little world. Then disaster happened. My parents were killed in an accident. I was left alone, with no relatives, to copewith this loss,' he said.

'My parents and I had agreed that I would be a professional golfer. Dad started teaching me the game at the age of eight. We had a three-hole layout cut from the large grove of pine trees in the middle of the farm. The holes were arranged in a way that could be played three different ways, making it a nine-hole array,' he said.

'Two families lived on the farm. They all worked for Dad, maintaining the place. Every morning, the two of us would play nine holes before I went to school, and then eighteen after coming home, before supper. Dad was a good golfer and teacher. I was taught to never give up, play every shot, and win. We had some mighty good rounds during the last year. I wanted to beat him, and he made me work hard on every shot. It was the best year of my life, but suddenly it was over; that part, anyway,' he said.

Dad filmed all my practice sessions, and we would go over theworkout, pointing out mistakes and the good shots. Those films were a Godsend afterward. I continued the same ritual every day but included playing at a country club regularly. I needed to establish an official handicap. I had formulated a plan for my life. he continued.

CHAPTER SEVEN

'I had visited Vegas that winter, trying to get over the depressionof my loss. I noticed the sports betting area and saw the odds being posted on the upcoming U.S. Open golf tournament. The favorites were all given odds to win, and all the others were groupedtogether under the same odds. My eyes, however, were glued to thechances given for an amateur to win. The odds were one thousand toone. Which meant you won one hundred thousand dollars on a one hundred-dollar bet.

'I went to all the casinos, and their odds were the same, except several of the small ones did not offer the amateur bet. I found one,the largest, and began placing bets on basketball and hockey games.I consistently achieved the best results with the same person each time. I waited until he was working and made small talk with him each time. My wagers were large because I needed him to get to know me. I did this for two weeks before laying the first one on the American Open golf tournament.

'My wager today, Mr. Smith, is one thousand dollars on an amateur to win the U.S. Open, he said. 'I want the same amount for the identical outcome on the British Open', Jack said.

Mr. Smith advised him that he would have to get his superior's approval for such a wager. He came back shortly with an okay. As he was entering the bet, he said that it was a curious one. 'Do you have someone in mind?' Mr. Smith asked.

'No, I just like the odds,' Jack answered.

'I lost the bet that year. Every few months, I returned for a couple of days and consistently placed my bets with Mr. Smith. The time for the golf open arrived, and I placed the same two wagers once again. I lost these, also.The next year, I bet and lost,' he said.

The fourth year he approached the betting window. Mr. Smith saw him coming and shook his head.

'You are a persistent young man. The same,' he asked.

'Yeah, one more time. Do you have odds on the same amateur winning both the Opens in the same year', Jack asked.

No, but I'll go see,' he said.

'While you are at it, find out what the limit would be on such a wager', Jack inquired.

He came back shortly, accompanied by two men. 'We wanted tosee the guy who has been placing these same bets over the years. Doyou believe you can win?' They asked.

'Well, I wouldn't be spending my money if I didn't, which is forsure. Plus, I love the odds, he said.

'The odds will be two thousand to one on the bet the same amateur will win the U.S. Open and the British Open this year. And you canbet any amount,' they said.

CHAPTER EIGHT

'I had made all these wagers over the years to get this chance. There was a limit before, and I had succeeded in getting it raised. Now was the time to go all in, so to speak,' Jack said.

'I want my wager to be five hundred thousand dollars on the bet that the same amateur golfer will win both the U.S. Open and the British Open this year, ' he said.

He put the large satchel on the counter. They counted the money and issued him his betting slip. He had the wager he wanted. Now, all he had to do was win two of the most famous golf tournaments in the world. But before he could do anything, he had to qualify for the American tournament. That is why they call it an 'Open. Any golfer with the required official handicap can enter these qualifying rounds. They reserve a certain number of places in the event for these winners.

CHAPTER NINE

'But first, I had to prepare for the possibility that someone might want to stop me from winning a billion dollars. I chose thelargest casino with the most investments in Las Vegas.

A small outfit could just declare bankruptcy, and it would be a hard, legal fight to get the pay-off. Yet, the larger one he chose was rumored to be owned by the mob, out of New York. They would not sit backand let me take their money without making an effort to stop me, maybe causing me to have an accident. Just a little one, to keep mefrom winning,' he said.

'So, I closed the family farm, and I, along with the two families, moved out. They were old friends of my father and my true, loyal backers. Through a corporation Dad had set up years ago, I bought a ranch in far west Texas. The men were officers in the company, and their names were on the deed. We all moved into these isolated, dilapidated buildings, which had been abandoned for years. We were miles and miles from any other humans, and it was exactly what wewanted, he said.

To avoid indicating occupancy, we maintained the original external appearance while renovating the interiors of the three houses.Anyone flying over would not be able to see how beautiful they wereon the inside. The same thing was done to the main barn. It was a largebuilding resembling an arena. I made it into a practice range where Icould use every club in my bag, hitting long shots against the far wall, which was completely covered by a net. The smaller building was turned into a parking garage, so we could keep all vehicles under cover.A full-sized eighteen-wheeler cattle trailer was used to haul supplies from a food distributor two hundred miles away for our phantom country store, he said.

'Also, the men made purchases of building materials in various towns, a long way from the ranch. We wanted to leave the appearance of an old homestead, barely livable, to the place, which was what it lookedlike.

With the small herd of prime cattle, pigs, chickens and vegetable garden, this was to be my long-range hideout, after I won', Jack said.

CHAPTER TEN

'I had my handicap at minus one, which allowed me to be a contestant for a spot in the U.S. Open. After I successfully won that entry into the tournament, I avoided all publicity until it began. I knew the casino had connected the results of my play to my bet. They had to be alerted to the possibility of me winning. Theelaborate means I had taken to get such a large wager accepted would now be evidence to them of a well-thought-out effort to take a billion dollars from them. I knew I had to be very careful from now on. And Imade plans to protect myself,' he said.

The ranch was meant to be my safe haven. All my efforts to conceal my presence there could be compromised, so I hadto construct a secure place on the ranch to retreat into. There was anold bunkhouse set away from the other structures. It already had a cellar, which we enlarged and fortified. We could defend ourselves from anything short of very big bombs when we finished with it, he said.

"I did not anticipate any issues at the U.S. Open, but I was prepared." By surrounding myself with men furnished by the best detective agency in the country, I kept out of the public's eye. My real work would be preparations for England. If I won the U.S. Open, thedanger would become real over there,' he said.

'I leased a large estate just miles from where the tournament was to be played. My name was on the paper, open to the world. One month before the play was to begin, a large party moved in, getting the place ready for my appearance,' he said.

'Months before, my guys had rented a cottage right across the street from the golf course. This had no connection to me in any way, but it would be our home. There was to be a large entourage arrivingat the estate, in darkened touring cars, unloading in the garage, while at the cottage, my caddy and I would await tee-time. And tea-time, British style. We could drive across the street and go for the gold, so to speak,' he said.

CHAPTER ELEVEN

You know the history of the U. S. Open. Dad had taught mewell, and my matches with him made me play under 'pressure' conditions all the time. Playing at the club was merely to establish my handicap, and I never went all-out there. Everythingalways pointed to this tournament, and I played really good golf. Iwas an unknown in the first round, so there was no crowd around me.I enjoyed the day very much, as my protective array of men was myaudience up to the final holes. Matters changed somewhat whenpeople began reacting to my low score, but it wasn't too bad. 'It will be different tomorrow,' I told my caddy.

'Sure enough, the fairway was lined with spectators and packed solid around the tee. I still was not concerned about my safety- yet.I felt sure any threats would likely come in England if I won the American Open. We had a good day of golf on this second day, but I was not going to engage with the media, so it was turned into a sournote because I did not make myself available. The same thing on the third day, with crowds getting larger and larger, and louder,' he said.

'During this round, I had instructed my lawyers to contact the FBIand set up a meeting after the day's golf was finished. The agency refusedbut set up a date the following week. I agreed to this, and I played thefinal eighteen holes and won the U. S. Open golf tournament,' he said.

The reporter had sat through Jack's narration, taking notes. Questions were forming in his inquisitive mind. He attempted to interrupt but was told the golfer's story would be finished first.

'I had planned very well ahead of the British Open to ensure mygood health would take me to the affair', Jack continued his tale.

'I was booked to sail on a tramp steamer out of New Orleans. Mymen used a dummy corporation to lease the vessel, and it was going to Scotland. I felt my measures should protect me, but if I could get theFBI involved, then all should go well. My reason given for the meetingwas that there was a threat from the mafia on my life, he said.

Since nothing had happened so far, they were not convinced. I had not told them of the wager. My trump card was that the government would receive over four hundred million dollars, in taxes, if I won thebet, he said.

Jack paused in his narrative, allowing the reporter to ask questions. 'You are telling an amazing story, Mr. Proctor. After all these years,

Why at this time? Has something happened?' Jim Carriage asked.

'Let me finish telling everything in the order events happened. I'llget to your question soon, Jack said.

'Right after the last putt sealed the victory for me at U.S. Open, Ihad the detective agency working for me to put out a rumor in NewYork City. I would be staying at a house in Queens for a visit with an oldfriend of my father's family. It was to be a very short meeting,' he said.

'We had staked out the neighborhood and rented another house just across the street from the one where our get-together was to beheld. We had people with cameras and mikes all over the place, fortwo blocks. We were setting a scene to get evidence for my appeal to the federal agency. The day of my supposed visit, we recorded two carscruising in front and back of the house I was to be in. One car was parkedseveral houses up the street. The other drove through the alley, slowly approaching. They saw that it looked empty as they passed and parked around the corner. Our cameras got a lot of good pictures of the fourmen in each of the cars, along with movies from different anglesand the photos of the license plates of the cars.

I met with the FBI and described our actions. I told him again,I felt certain the mob had put out a 'hit' order on me. I demandeda meeting with the director in person if they identified the men looking for me in those two cars as Mafia. Also, I told them I had further proof as to why this order was given. Jack continued.

'Why would these guys be gunning for you, Mr. Proctor. We have run a full investigation on you and cannot find anything to suggest such an operation is planned by the mafia', the Fed asked.

CHAPTER TWELVE

'The next day, I presented the head man a photocopy of the betting slip and made my case.' 'Two reasons you should be interested in this matter. First, I believe my life is in danger. Second, the bet you are holding is for about four hundred million 'tax' dollars if I win in England. I will win, Mr. Director, but I have to stay healthy,' Jack said.

'Plans have been laid out to keep me out of harm's way, but I need your help to assure me I will participate all the way to victory. If you decline to protect me, and I win, I will declare myself a Brit and pay the taxes to them. I'll let you two countries fight over the money, but I doubt you'll get a penny. It is up to you people to help keep me in the game. I think my plan will work, but your assistance should guarantee it, he said.

'The men recorded in my scheme were all identified as members of the mob family associated with the casino where I made the wager in question. I was told several years later that my information had been confirmed through another mob family the FBI was monitoring at the time. They talked about a furious, murderous rage the head man in Nevada went into one day. Two men working at one of the large casinos in Vegas were beaten up by him in front of a lot of witnesses. And it was about a large wager the house had accepted. The FBI also had a report from the field about an effort to lay-off this bet after the American Open was over. No one would take any of it, and this was the real reason for the rampage in Vegas. The casino would stand to lose the entire amount alone. The normal procedure for a big wager is to sell parts of it to other houses. That minimized the risk. The two guys who approved the bet decided it was impossible to lose, so they sat on it. After my winning the first of the two opens, they could not get any other casino to take any part of the wager, he said.

'Anyhow, the director decided to help me. They got us to England on official visas and furnished security, along with the involvement of Scotland Yard. They identified a number of suspects at the British event. You know the excitement that was stirred up, and the golf officials were told only there had been a threat against one of the contestants. They wanted to exclude me from playing because of it, but both theAmerican and British governments would not allow them to cancel me. I understand the two made an agreement about the taxes. Moneydoes talk, doesn't it', Jack proclaimed.

CHAPTER THIRTEEN

'We are meeting here because I want it to remain a secret where I have been living these many years. I will take youthere, but only if we can blindfold you, Mr. Carraige. I have a few things to show you, which will make my story complete. Doyou want to go? Jack asked.

The reporter, Jim Carraige, had sat taking notes during the golfer's presentation and explanations of the events that had transpired so many years ago. His questions had been answered as the tale unfolded. There had been rumors of such a bet, way back then. Yet nothing approaching what Jack Proctor had revealed. The newspaper man realized he had the 'story' of the century. His many years of work were going to pay off, big time, he thought.

'I certainly do want to go, Mr. Proctor. Will you place any restrictions on any articles I write?' he said.

'Yes, there will be some details I will demand you withhold, for safety's sake. I'll cover everything with you later,' Jack said.

They entered the ranch through an old, ornate cast-iron gateway. As they entered the grounds, his mask was removed. The convoy traveled several miles on a road which had no ruts and was not used often, it was plain to see. The buildings came into view, and Jim was struck by the sight. It was a picture out of 'The Grapes of Wrath' movie, except there was no evidence anyone lived here. Everything looked a hundred years old, right down to a hitching post next to the porch entrance to the 'big house.'

But everything changed the moment they stepped through the front door. From the past to the present in an instant. The interior was modern and lavishly furnished but retained the rustic decor of the Western ranch house. They were greeted by a whole bunch of people, allrushing to hug the men as each came through the door.

CHAPTER FOURTEEN

'Allow me to introduce everyone. Over here is the Hancock family. Along with the Smith clan, right here were the two families who have been intertwined with the Proctors for so many years, Jack said.

'I grew up with these folks, and both agreed to move with me tothis place. I haven't gotten to this group over here because they area special band of people. The beautiful Lady is June, the daughter of Mr. and Mrs. Smith. Next is Mary, and then Susan. They are thedaughters of Mr. and Mrs. Jack Proctor. Yes, sir, my lovely childrenand wife. June and I have known one another all our lives, and we fell in love after my parents died. June made it possible for me to live through the dark days afterward. She loved my mother and dad, and we grieved together. I knew it was loving the first time we hugged each other, but I never spoke about how I felt. She told me later that she fell in love with me at about the same time. It was several years before wefinally confronted each other pertaining to those feelings. We were married the following year, much to the joy of both families. We were truly one big happy group,' he said.

'We have been, sort of, under the witness protection program allthese years. The FBI found evidence that a contract had been put out for me by the crime family, and this fact connected them to the casino in Vegas. The Don of the group had not withdrawn the 'hit' order, even after I collected the bet. He blamed me for the government attention he was getting. And his mandate led us to establish this ranch as our'safe house,' as it were. No one found us, so why am I talking to you,now, you ask,' he said.

CHAPTER FIFTEEN

'Well, the "Godfather" died last year, and the feds got word my business with the mob died with him. I have waited almost a year to try to make sure. I don't want to endanger these people, so it is why I have asked you to keep this ranch out of your story. Not the history of the place, just the location. We have very strong defenses here, which will remain secret, and we will not venture out into the world just yet,' he said.

'This interview with you is sort of my -' coming out. We will be careful, but we are finally free, I hope. I am not sure we will be forgotten. Money speaks very loudly to these people, just as does their honor system. My incident touches on both those sacred subjects, he said.

Maybe I'll enter some golf tournaments. I have kept my game into top-notch form, and I'm relatively young. Plus, we are filthy rich', he said.

The reporter and his editor were going over the first article about to be considered for printing. The main topic was how much could they include in this installment.

'You are going to be famous, Mr. Carraige. We must be careful that this story is presented the right way since both the government and te mafia are involved. Some very highly placed people managed to keep this away from you. It would have been made public years ago otherwise. I am going to call the FBI and alert them. They still have an active file concerning Mr. Proctor, if he is under their witness program,' he said.

The FBI agent sat across from the editor and alongside Jim Carraige in the newspaper office.

'I'm glad you asked for this meeting instead of talking on the phone about this matter. This is still a very sensitive case, even after all these years. We are aware of the session you had with Mr. Proctor. Did he arrange the interview, Jim?', the federal agent asked.

'Yes, he called me. I guess he knew of my continued interest in this matter. At least, it is what he told me. I got the feeling he thought things were pretty well finished between him and the mob. Does theFBI think the guy is in danger? He gave me the story and permission to run it, as long as I left out a few details, Jim said.

'I wanted to clear the articles with you guys, before we go any further', the editor spoke up.

'Here is all I can tell you about our active file concerning Jack Proctor. It has been over a year since the 'Don' left us. We have heard nothing to indicate that the family still seeks revenge. Everything points to a closed case, but we can't be sure. Therefore, we are going to keep aneye on the matter. I have been advised to tell you it is clear for you air the story, as far as we are concerned,' the agent said.

CHAPTER SIXTEEN

Jim Carraige was overwhelmed by the response to the first segment of the story. There was a whole generation of Americanand British people who knew very little about Jack Proctor.

Many had read of his exploits, but only from Jim's articles once a year.The fact that so much money was involved, along with the crime families,made it a sensational expose.

There was a loud and determined group who demanded more details. One story about the mafia being located in Vegas was enough to light a fire under law enforcement efforts to combatsuch activities. The widow of the Don, Mrs. Carpo, was now in control of the casino. She sent letters to the local newspapers with statements about the operations.

'No illegal activities have ever been run in our business. My husband completely left any other type of venture many years ago. We have had only local people working for us, with most employed fora long time. I will continue the operation as an honest enterprise and hope to provide jobs for a wonderful group of men and women, she wrote.

Jim soon realized the epic tale of Jack Proctor had become 'old news. He included this latest episode in his large file under his name. The next chapter will probably be added in a year unless something new develops before then. The reporter hoped all these years of searching for the facts in this story had been worth it. Time would tell, and it was about to strike the 'high-noon' hour.

'FORE'-Warned
Book II

CHAPTER ONE

The Don was surrounded by his family as he lay in his bed. Heknew he only had a short time left on this earth, and the fact reflectedon the faces of those gathered around. He was ready to go because old age had brought him to this moment instead of the actions of themany people who wanted to see him dead. Mr. Sam Carpo had liveda life completely under the banner of his other 'family'- the so-called mafia. It was very important to him that he depart this world on his terms and not through any act of someone else. There was enough evidence among his kinfolk here of those left behind who had lost loved ones and family members due to the bloody war he helped foment. Of hisfour children, only one stood before him. The children and widowsof the three sons who had died were here to remind him and their mother of just how much they missed them.

Andy stood alone at the side of the bed. He loved his father, andthe sight of the once-robust man made him very sad. He never was involved in the affairs of the 'family' because of his mother. She had required that her youngest child be excluded from the responsibilities and tasks that her three older sons had undertaken. She even went so far as to name him Anthony Smithe, which was her maiden name. Anthony was not goingto be connected in any way to his father's business. Everything went quite well with that arrangement, until the episode of the 'bet'.

Many years earlier, the family had decided to invest in a casino in Vegas. The Don wanted to get out of the normal activities connected to the mob. He believed gambling was the only reliable way to avoid the racketeering practiced by other families in the east. He knew the feds were going to crack down hard someday soon, and he took everything out west. The move was made during the first stages of the opening of gambling in a big way in Las Vegas. He came under the grandfather clauses when strict regulations began to weed out the late entries, leaving his operation the lone survivor from the New York gangs. He adhered to all regulations and eventually managed the most prosperous and well-operated casino in town. It was this fact that led Jack Proctor to choose this site as the location to place his infamous wager of five hundred thousand at two thousand-to-one odds, which was that an amateur golfer would win both the US Open and the British Open golf tournaments in the same year. The casino's mistake was accepting the bet without laying off part of it. This is a practice used by all gambling operations on large or high-odds bets, where they sell a portion to other houses. The two men responsible for these errors decided it was a good choice to make the wager, so they kept it all in-house.

CHAPTER TWO

Not only did the casino lose, but their futile efforts to keep Jack from winning by hurting him led the FBI to go after the Don. This was compounded by putting a contract out on the golfer and the beating of the men who allowed the bet to be made. This triggered an FBI raid on the family's headquarters. A fierce gun battle ensued, ending up with the three sons of the Don's being killed.

The family laid all blame for this tragedy at the feet of Jack Proctor. It became the first priority to punish the man, to kill him. For twenty years, they searched for him, but to no avail. Now, the head man lay at death's bed, with no one to continue the quest. However, he was not going to give up. He instructed everyone around him to start the rumor that the feud would end with his death. He then asked everyone to leave the room he was in, except his one remaining son.

'Anthony, your mother and I have always agreed to keep you out of the family business. You were younger by a lot of years because we had decided not to have any more children, but along came this surprise, you. We both welcomed you as a gift from God, and you did not disappoint us. We love you very much. Now, I am going to ask you to do something for me after I die. I don't want you to tell anyone about what I am about to say. Promise me you won't talk to anyone ever, Anthony, he asked.

'I won't tell anyone, Dad,' he said.

'All of our troubles began because of that bet Jack Proctor made at our casino. He planned everything so very well, and our people did their best to help him. I had kept us legal here in Vegas, away from the eastern families and their rackets, until the feds were brought in due to one guy. I know you will remind me of my actions that were really dumb moves. I would not have tried to stop him if I had any idea of his plans to bring the FBI into the picture. It was a stupid decision on my part, as hindsight now shows me. Which brings us here, son. You are the one remaining heir of mine. I have put the word out to everyone to forget and forgive the whole affair. For the world, I say that, but to you, I want to get the man. I want you to promise you will find him and kill him. Your father asks for this last wish to be honored. he said.

39

CHAPTER THREE

All his life, Anthony had been shielded from his father's business. His mother had insisted most of his up-bringing be left in her hands. Since he was so much younger than his three brothers, it wasn't hard to channel him away from their influence. He was a late, accidental addition to their family, and his mother spoiled him badly. It was fine with everyone else for him not to be involved with the others. Now, his father had shocked him beyond words by his request. No, it was more than just a mere request. His father was making this far more than asking a favor. It was a mandate.

Nothing in his life had prepared Andy for what his father was asking him to do. As he listened, he was thankful for the dim lighting in the room and his dad's condition; otherwise, the shocked look on his face would have shown his utter dismay.

Dad, I have never been included in your business. You know how I feel about any type of violence. I have always avoided confrontations. Mother never let me roughhouse with my brothers. She would step in and take me away from them when they were playing together and matters got physical. I wanted to stay and be a part of the action, so to speak. This feeling about not being a man eroded my confidence, so I overcame such emotions by being good at the sports I took up. None were 'contact' sports, but as you know, I am a good golfer and swimmer. Can't you handle this matter another way? You scare me to death, asking me to do this,' he said.

The look on the old man's face told Anthony all he needed to know about how much this meant to his dad. He immediately changed his tune and knelt by the bed.

'I see how much you want me to do this for you. I promise you it will be done, Father. Forget all about it. You don't need to worry anymore', he said.

Andy decided that he had plenty of time. After the death of his father, he would have to deal with the request, but it could be years, or maybe never, he thought.

Two days later, his father died. For his mother's sake, he could not display the relief he felt. The emotions he showed were of grief, but inside, there was another part of him reacting in a much different way. He had enrolled earlier at an out-of-state university upon receiving a golf scholarship. He was going to devote himself to this sport he loved and try to make a career out of it. Now, he would be even more dedicated, and he would put aside as long as he could this albatross his dad had hung around his neck. He knew the matter had to be addressed someday, but he would worry about Jack Proctor tomorrow.

CHAPTER FOUR

Jack Proctor had not been idle during the twenty years of his exile. A very large part of the money he won wagering on winning the U.S. Open and the British Open golf tournaments the same yearas an amateur went into a Swiss numbered account. He never touchedit; he only used the interest it generated. The remainder was split between thetwo families who had helped him survive the mob's efforts to keep himfrom winning. They had joined in a joint adventure, buying a large ranchnearby.

Vegas had always fascinated Jack. Here was a town, mainly with one main street, which was lined with gambling houses of all sizes and shapes. Irrigated and made possible by the huge dam only a few miles away. An oasis in a vast semi-arid wasteland. He saw an ad in the local newspaper, showing a large tract a few miles out of town that was upfor sale. The following year, he visited the site. It had not been sold.His vivid imagination showed him a beautiful golf course among thedunes and ravines, along with a majestic clubhouse, surrounded by cottages, swimming pools, and tennis courts. He promised to buy the plot of land.

Using the same corporation, he directed the families to purchase the place. If his wager became a reality, they would develop it one day into a resort. He felt the town would eventually come out to this location, making it a valuable asset. It was a long shot investment, for sure.

This was in addition to the ranch Jack had bought before his infamous adventure. He planned everything toward going into hiding with these people who had been with his father for so many years. This place was where everyone came to live and where he had brought the reporter,Jim Carraige, the day he came out of hiding. It was almost twenty years keeping away from the public's eyes, to avoid the revenge foremost in the plans of the mob family.

'We need to have this place', William Smith stated. 'There is an abandoned mining town on the property we can resurrect and use asour home base. Our cover would be that mine was going to be opened. There is a general store, a hotel with a dining area we could make into a cafe, and several buildings we could use as a bank and school, he said.

'I suspect we will be traced to our location here, so we need another safe -haven. We have the kids away in a private school far from here, which we bought years ago. They will be able to finish grade schoolthere and go on to college wherever they choose. Each of our familieshas a resident at the school, as you know. The children are happy there,and the place is secure,' Jack said.

Everyone worked on the renovations of the town, taking one building at a time. They also shored up the mineshaft with steel and concrete. It was a level shaft, going deep into the mountain, so it was easy to modernize the place. This would be their 'fortress' if they were attacked.

'I know you guys think I am paranoid about our well-being, but weare going to be safe - not sorry,' he would say over and over again.

The marriage of Jack Proctor and June Smith had produced two beautiful daughters. June was William and Betty Smith's only child. They were one of the two families who joined Jack when they moved into the ranch. Susan was the youngest and became his golfing buddy early on. From the age of four, she took to the game, much to Jack's delight. The older Mary played also, but she never had the 'fever' Susan did. All three would play by the hour, much to the joy of June. Jackhad insisted from the beginning that they would play only serious golf.Jack would instruct as they played, much to the dismay of Susan. This was fun for her, and teaching got in the way.

When Mary finished high school and was preparing to enter college, Jack and June realized the girls would have to be told the full story of Jack's earlier adventures. No one had ever mentioned the affair, and it was decided to put off addressing the issue until the girls were ready to go out into the world. Now was the time.

CHAPTER FIVE

Jack wanted everyone to be present at the meeting he called. Mostof the immediate Smith family had moved to the ranch, and alongwith the Jordan family, there was a good-sized crowd. Sam and Wilma Jordan were the second family that had come to the ranch withthem. Their group consisted of both sets of parents but no children. Thatmeant only Mary and Susan would be leaving the ranch.

'I have asked you all here, as we will be preparing the girls for their adventure into the world, so to speak. As you all recall, we have always requested no mention be made of why we are all here at this ranch, he said. Turning to his children, Jack told his story:

CHAPTER SIX

Both the girls adored their father. He had always displayed manly traits to them and had given them almost everything they had ever asked for. Now, they were finding out about his heroics as a champion golfer. They were dumb founded.

'I had to keep this from you until you were old enough to understand the need for this secrecy. All of us are in danger since these people can get to me through any one of you. Now, Mary is ready for college, and she must leave the safety of this ranch. Thank you for going along with our request for you to go to our choice of universities. I know this was difficult for you since the State college was where you wanted to go. Your mom and I couldn't tell you the real reason, but now you know. We have made arrangements for your security at the private school that we could not do otherwise. They have an excellent golf program if you decideto play. Now, don't get any ideas in your pretty head that I was looking ahead when Susan would enroll, young lady. Well, I did think about it, to be honest,' he said.

From the time the girls could remember, they had asked why their last name was Smith and not Proctor, as their mother and father were called. Now, they knew. This day had been anticipated a long time ago. They looked around at the circle of friends surrounding them and realized they all were under the same umbrella of security throughout the ranch.

The high, extra-strong fence, the restrictions placed on where they could not go. Plus, the frequent helicopters that appeared out of nowhere, always flying down that fence line. They were mostly only heard because the property limits were a long way from the houses.

Little did they know of the base camp and airport in the foothillsto the south, within the ranch. This camp was home to four militarygrade helicopters, five regular ones, and over twenty highly trained ex special forces men, all on ready alert.

'We are not in danger at this ranch, young ladies,' he explained. 'The FBI keeps me informed about what is going on outside, as we are sort of under a witness protection program. This will include watching over you in school. You won't ever see them, but they will be close. We are going to have to reveal the presence of this place, however, as I plan to meet the press, so to speak, very soon, he said.

Jack brought them up to date regarding the death of the Don, who owned the casino where he had placed his infamous bet.

'The FBI has informed me the contract on my life, which has existed all these years, has been cancelled. It sounds like good news, but I have been leery about the news. I am concerned why this information was almost broadcasted to the world. Someone seemed anxious to tell the world. However, a year has passed, and there has not been anything to make the feds think otherwise. I want this new place to be our home, just in case,' he said.

CHAPTER SEVEN

It had been over a year since his father's death, but Anthony had not heard anything about the man he had promised to do away with. Not a word, which did not bother him. He had started his college golf career and had done very well. He always thought it was ironic, him taking up the game that had caused his family so much grief. He really did not think a lot about the matter since it had been a busy year for him. Yet, it always burst out, front and center, when he got ready to fall asleep at night. He wanted to contact one of his dad's close friends and ask him to take care of the guy, but he had been warned not to involve anyone else, as it could easily get back to the FBI.

Any alert the hit was still active would end the effort before it ever could begin. Passing the ordeal off was not possible; he always concluded every night before drifting into sleep. This is where the affair stood as he started his second year on the golf team.

CHAPTER EIGHT

Susan's mother and sister drove with her on the trip to their school. Her dad could not come along because he might be recognized.

'I sure hope this mess gets fixed before the golf season begins. This is not how I figured my college career would start. Maybe we canget Dad to grow a beard, and we can disguise him, she said.

They all went to the coach's office to meet the head man. The school did not have a separate tutor for the girls, so the practices would becoed. They met the one coach, and since mother approved of him, everything went well.

'I have studied your swing on the films you sent me, and you have been taught very well. Who is the person responsible', the coach asked?

'My father is the only one who has ever instructed me. We have a nice layout on our ranch where Mary and I played with Dad, and he demanded a whole lot from us. Our practices and play were intenseand fun, Susan said.

From the looks and body stances the three women assumed, the coach knew not to inquire further about the man who knew how to teach golf, at least to this young lady. He knew the older sister attendedlast year but did not try out for the team.

'Golf does not interest me nearly as much as it does Susan, nor am I as good as she is. Dad's talent rubbed off on her,' Mary said.

Now, that little tidbit of information made the meeting he had attended with the president of the school more relevant and meaningful to him. He was told not to seek any further information on the familyof Mary and Susan Smith than what was on the paper he handed him.

'They are a big donor and are very private. You are not to discussthem with anyone. I mean 'anyone,' Coach. Your future here would be shaky if you violate these instructions. You are in complete control ofSusan's golf participation at this school. Just don't go beyond what is necessary to do your job,' he said.

CHAPTER NINE

Susan's golfing skills became apparent when the team had theirfirst practice session. Even the guys stopped to watch her swing. The young lady was so engrossed in her efforts that she didn'tnotice most of the players admiring her routine. She was all business. Her style showed she had been trained toward an aggressive approach to the game. The coach and several of the men commented about it.'I have only seen this in the women who play on the tour', one of theplayers said.

'Yeah, she is going to be fun to watch, and I can see how to reallytest her game. Bob, I want you to partner with her in today's round.Since you are our number three player, you will be up against Jim and Richard, our top-ranked men, the coach said. 'Susan will be using thesame tees as you. That makes the match uneven, but I want to see howshe plays under pressure. I don't want any bets made today, none whatsoever, do you understand? No outside pressure at all, the Coachsaid.

The foursome was walking up the last fairway, followed by a pretty large gallery. During the round, students joined some of the other players watching the exciting golf. They were all square in the match, much to the chagrin of Susan's opponents and the delight of everyone else, including the coach. It did not matter how this final hole wouldcome out. He was overjoyed by the play of all four players.

'I am going to have her competing every day with the men's team.

They bring out the best in each other,' he said.

It would not surprise this coach if this pretty young lady became a champion. The suspense was growing, however, about the person who had taught her so well. He eagerly awaited the season to meet his favorite player's parents.

CHAPTER TEN

Trouble was brewing in the ranks of the organization left by the departed 'Don.' All the men had loved their boss and moaned with him at the death of his sons. It was expected that the last one, Anthony, would take over the reins and continue his father's traditions.However, they had been informed the young man was headed off tocollege, and the widow was selling the casino and abandoning all connections with the business. This was bad news to the two top menleft in charge by the Don before he died. The casino was a big success, and it was their hard work that brought it through the debacle causedby the 'bet', as everyone called Jack Proctor's wager, which caused all the turmoil. The men demanded a meeting with the wife to present her with the problems her actions were causing.

'If there is any change in the ownership of the casino, the State will revoke the license. All the workers, their families, and your husband's staff, i.e., his 'soldiers', will be set adrift. This is the oldest and best-run operation in town and the only one with the grandfather clause that keeps us open. The corporation that owns it was set up to exclude the family from ownership. We want to buy you out and keep everything the same,' they said. 'We thought Andy would take his father's place as the new Don.' We know he never participated,and we would run the operation, but his presence would continue the dynasty, so to speak. That would allow everyone, including the other 'families, the feds, and the State agencies, to let the place keep running,' the man said.

'I will agree to do as you ask, except for my son's involvement in any way. But I will not sell it to you. I am going to retain control of thecasino. The operations are yours. I make one stipulation. You must runit legally. Take everything away from Vegas that could cause problemswith the law. If you promise to allow Andy to do his own thing, thenwe have a deal', the woman said.

CHAPTER ELEVEN

The young man in question was unaware of all the background activities on his behalf. He was getting ready to begin his secondyear at the university. After his stellar work on the golf team, he was named the captain, and he was focused only on his play and hisstudies. The team's first meeting was with three other schools, one of thembeing a small private institution.

'We included them because they supposedly have a good group, especially on the women's side,' the coach said.

All the golfers were on the practice tee, men and women. As competitors are prone to do, Anthony and his fellow players were sizing up the field as they warmed up. It was quite apparent one young ladywas getting most of the male's attention, both for her 'form' as a golferand as a woman. Andy could not take his eyes off the girl. He thoughtshe was the prettiest female he had ever seen.

'Andy, are you here to practice or to gawk at the young lady?' his coach said. He saw his captain halt and stare at the girl. He had also noted that she had looked in Anthony's direction several times, with more than a casual glance. He could not blame either young person. Each was a fine example of humanity, but he had to remind his player about the business at hand.

It was a very good match for everyone's opening outing for the year. Anthony played well enough to win his contests. He casually questioned each of his opponents about who the young lady was and how she developed such a smooth, sound golf swing. They all laughed at him.

'So, it is her 'golf swing' you are interested in,' they all answered. 'Nothing to do with her 'smooth, sound body.' Plus, her beautiful face, huh?

Tony could only sheepishly grin and admit it was not just idle curiosity on his part.

CHAPTER TWELVE

Without being too obvious, Andy inched his way to where Susan was standing as the teams mingled in the clubhouse after everyone had finished their rounds. She was aware of the man and made it easy for them to meet. There was a mutual attraction between them, and it did not go unnoticed. She was too young for most of the men in the room, but that did not deter the looks of admiration or attentiveness toward her. The talk was all golf and school when they finally met, with nothing else mentioned. They wished each other luck, and Andy told her he hoped to see her again.

'I plan to play in the state tournament. Maybe I'll see you there,' she said. Anthony wanted to ask her for her phone number but sensed her reluctance to advance the meeting beyond casual social lines. Her demure gesture toward a possible future meeting would have to do, he thought.

The exchange between Susan and Andy did not escape the notice of two men standing in the room. The detective agency had assigned these agents to keep a protective eye on Susan. Jack Proctor had waited this long to allow his girls to venture out into the world due to his concern for their safety. He felt the threat that had hung over them for so long was now gone, yet he still was worried. Their last names were different, and there was nothing to connect them, but he retained the agency just in case. They knew who Andy was from the beginning but felt no need to alert the father. However, this display of mutual attraction between the pair was something else. They provided their boss with a report and several photos. Everything was forwarded to Jack within an hour, and he acted on the information immediately.

CHAPTER THIRTEEN

Jack called the FBI contact assigned to him and explained whathad happened. 'We do not have a lot to tell you about the Don's last son, except he never was associated with the business. Now, he seems to be the figurehead the family is using to run the casino, along with his mother. The place is a cash cow and is being operatedlegally in every way. We have one source in the inner circle, though,who tells us the two men are the real bosses and unhappy Anthony didnot take his father's place, calling him a traitor. Nothing, however, toindicate he is anything but a student who met a pretty girl. There couldbe a lot of resentment remaining against you by these chiefs, whichcould be dangerous to your family, the FBI agent said.

The game of golf can bring both positive and negative outcomes simultaneously. I am not going to say a word to Susan about this. Let matters move along at their own pace, and we will watch from the sidelines, so to speak. I will be at the state tournament and will use the event to come out in the open. We will see how thingswork out, for sure, Jack said.

CHAPTER FOURTEEN

The school's golf program was drastically altered by their unexpected success. They were scheduled to play second tier teams due to theirsize and being a private institution, but the coach had received an invite changing everything. One of the better schools had been declared ineligible due to the misconduct of several of their players. They had to dropout of an important event, making room for the little boys and girls of thesmall private school for a chance to challenge the elites.

When Anthony heard Susan was going to be coming to town, hewas overjoyed. He had kept up with her team's success and followed their play in the media, especially hers. Her picture was on the newsseveral times, and he would sit, just looking. 'I must be in love', he toldhimself. His roommate caught him admiring her and told him that was a sure sign. He passed it off by saying he just thought she was pretty.

'Of course, you do. I do, too, but I'm not drooling over her. The best thing to do, Andy, is admit it and see what you can do about the matter,' he said.

That was the spark that set him on his life's quest for Susan Smith.

He would give it a shot and hope for the best.

CHAPTER FIFTEEN

On the day of the golf meet, Susan and Andrew met in the practice tees area. It was a casual and light-hearted occasion they both enjoyed. There was a rule both coaches had for their players against too much contact with opposing teams, especially between thesexes, so the meeting was short and sweet, to use a pun. Anthony looked her straight in the eye and said, 'I'll see you later.'"Certainly," she responded with a smile.

It was the best of everything for a lot of people. The spectators enjoyed the good play. The golfers had fun, some more than others,and none as much as Anthony and Susan. Both played very well, andthey had a couple of meaningful moments together. Tomorrow would be the final day of the meet. They had managed to see each other after dinner. There was hope, Andy thought, as they parted with a light kiss.

Several pairs of watchful eyes took everything in. A new observer had been added, as the intrigue intensified, behind the scenes. The East Coast families had put Anthony under surveillance several months ago, and these romantic encounters were noted and photographed. The FBI was really interested after a known capo from the Manhattan area showed up and was caught filming the kids. Then, there were the private eyes working for Jack Proctor. Susan and Andy had started something, but no one knew what it was, except it was evident it stemmed fromthe distant past. Alarm bells were sounding in Jack's camp and at FBI headquarters. The mob was up to no good.

CHAPTER SIXTEEN

Everything was running quite well at the casino, much to the reliefof the two bosses. The fact they did not own the place botheredthem very much, but they could not find any way to change matters. Money was coming in from this place and their other activities.They were unaware these successes were drawing the attention of the east coast families until a group of the hierarchy of those clans showedup in town and asked for a meeting. 'Asked' was a little misleadingto describe the summons. Maybe 'demand' would better portray their intent.

They wasted little time in passing on to the two men the reason for this highly unusual confab. It had to do with the casino deal theyarranged concerning the Don's family. There was no warning of theircoming. First, they landed at a place that could barely be called anairport. It was an old airstrip in the desert that had not been used in years. Second, word of the get-together had been brought to themby a currier, with instructions not to use any electronic device for communications. Third, come to the location given by roundaboutroutes, using evasive tactics. Third, no one else was to be told of thismeeting.

The two men sitting in front of this imposing array of gentlemenwere visibly nervous. Nothing was said to ease their discomfort, and noone was smiling.

'Reports are coming in about your operations that greatly disturbus. We want to hear your story first hand, and its importance is why weare here. So, let's hear your story, starting with how you two came out ontop after the Don's passing,' the man said.

They told how everything went down, which was already knownby the visitors. They passed the test, so they got to the reason for them being here.

'We want to take over the casino without changing any of the paperwork. This must happen. We have come up witha plan to make this happen. The widow is the key to this wholething. The license goes if the ownership changes, and none of us couldget a new one. So, the lady has to stay as the figurehead. There is a way to make her look the other way and let us run the show. Anthony is the bait. His mother will do anything to protect her boy. Threats against him could be thwarted only by completely altering his lifestyle. Making him give up everything he is now doing- school, golf,friends', the man said.

One of the other men spoke up. 'The question is making both Andy and his mother believe the threat is real. There has to be an exampleset. They had the photos of Anthony and Susan, and it was clear theycared for each other. They would hurt the young lady with the promiseof much worse to follow if the mother did not cooperate. The next stepwould be for them to harm her son, the man said.

This was the plan they agreed on.

CHAPTER SEVENTEEN

When the individuals from the casino entered the room, they were searched for weapons and electronic devices.

'Let me see those hearing aids,' the searcher demanded. He checked them and announced they were all right. Unbeknown to everyone, below the hearing aid in the right ear, deeper in the canal, was a recording device that was activated and became a part of the hearing aid when it was inserted deep enough to contact it. Everything that was happening in their meeting was in the FBI's hands the next day. The man needed an insurance policy, as he sensed dangerous events were about to happen.

'I believe Anthony is genuine, but I can't be sure,' the fed stated. 'He could be ready to avenge his father', the head man of the private eye company said.

Jack listened, but he had formed a plan to find out in a hurry. 'We are all going to the golf event tomorrow. I want to walk out on the first tee with Susan and be introduced as her father, just as Anthony is set to start. I want you all to observe his reaction. If he knew who I am, he would be deeply shocked. It will be a dead giveaway; he is not just the son of the Don but also is involved with me in some way. "The match will conclude, after which we can engage in a brief discussion," he stated.

CHAPTER EIGHTEEN

Andy's foursome was getting ready to come to the starting area when the announcer, instead of directing them to the tee-box, invited a couple to come to the microphone. 'You all know Susan, and now I want to introduce you to her father, Jack Proctor,' he said.

The shock Anthony felt as he watched the two walking forward was overwhelming. He instantly recognized the man he had sworn to kill. That was bad enough, but for him to be Susan's father almost brought him to his knees. Only a few people in the crowd noticed his anguish, but those folks recorded the whole scene on film. To make matters worse, Jack turned and looked him dead in the eyes, with a wry grinon his face. Some of the spectators had noticed and assumed this was a father seeing his daughter's possible boyfriend, but Anthony saw this as a statement. His expression indicated recognition.

This was only the second appearance in over 22 years for the champion golfer. This excited the crowd, for sure. Added to the moment were his ties toSusan and Mary. The three people walked hand-in-hand to the applause of everyone. They were joined by a large group as Andy's foursome started their round of golf.

CHAPTER NINETEEN

There was extra security around the final green as Anthony finished play. He was immediately led to the clubhouse, along with his mother. A large group of men were waiting for them. They introduced themselves and got right down to the business at hand.

'This is an urgent matter which pertains to you both,' the FBI leader said. 'We know Susan and her father have both been singled out as targets of your casino operations. We are going to play a tape recorded at a meeting of your two top men there and many higher-ups fromthe East Coast crime families. When we are finished, I think you both willwant to talk to us, he said.

Susan was seated at the back with her sister. She was still in a state of shock at learning about Andy's family. She was not really angry, and the look on the young man's face was so sad it made her want to comfort him. She pondered their future as she studied him. They were a long way from being a couple, but there was a special feeling between them, which was real.

The recording was received by some as very bad and by others as good news. It made the course of action an easy choice for Andy and his mother. He immediately told them of his father's request, much to the sorrow of his mother. Her bitterness at her husband's efforts to bring her son into his obsession, even as he lay on his deathbed, was intense.

'I placated him at the moment but never made any move to carryout his demand. Now, I find out the woman I love is his daughter. I am crushed beyond words,' Anthony said.

Tears came to her eyes as she heard Andy express his words of endearment. She truly liked the guy but had been shocked to learn of his connection to her father's problems, not to mention his promise to harm him. No one but her father knew where this was headed. With his arms around his family, he made this announcement to the mother and son.

'I am offering you a place of refuge. Our home has been our bastion of safety for a long time. Now, we offer you its protection, until the authorities can take these scumbags out', he said. Not everyone agreed this was a solution, but it was a well-received gesture.

CHAPTER TWENTY

'I don't think it is a good idea to go with them, Andy. We will be amongst people who have lived for many years in fear of 'our' family. I cannot imagine that all the anxiety and worry will be forgotten so easily. You really have disappointed me, young man. I spent my wholemarried life fighting your father and his 'family.' It was my naggingwhich led him to the casino business, and away from the mob in NewYork', she said.

'You could have told me about his death-bed request against an innocent man. It would have been dismissed immediately, but you chose to keep it from me. I would have sold the business years ago ifI had known about it. None of this should have happened, Anthony.So, now I have to go to Vegas and separate us completely from the past. You have to remain under the protection of the authorities until I get itdone. Then, we can talk about our future. Right now, everything aboutour lives is at a standstill,' she said.

'Mother, put yourself in my shoes, please. I loved my father. I satthere when he asked me to kill a human being, shocked beyond words.You should have seen the look on his face as I protested his request.I could not refuse his wish. I knew I must not lie to him, so I truly made him a promise. I have been tormented ever since by my decision,Mom, Tony said.

Reba Carpo returned to the casino and began organizing the staff since the two lead men who had been running the placewere gone. With help from most of those who had worked for her husband for years, she got everything going smoothly again. Herplans were to put the place up for sale, but the more she was aroundall those folks, the more her thoughts moved to accept the notion that thecasino was a nice business.

'I have decided to run the casino, Tony. You will continue in school and pursue golf as a career if this is what you desire. I want you to be totally separated from the business. There may be overtures from theNew York people to buy us out, but I do not believe we will be harmed physically, his mother said.

'Since the license cannot be a part of selling the place, right now,we don't have a lot to offer. We are behind in modernizing becauseyour father wanted to keep the original building and decor. Most ofthe people working for us were loyal to your father, with many of them expressing relief by my decision to take over, she said.

'Four people are remaining who worked real closely with the guys who were running your business, Mrs. Carpo. There was definitelya close connection between them we all picked up on, the head of security stated.

"We were indeed surprised that they did not depart with their colleagues," the supervisor remarked.

'They work in the crew who transfer the money boxes at the tables and game sites down to the vault. We have cameras on them at all times, right down to the counting room in the vault below. They have continued to do a good job, but they pretty much keep to themselves. I have added several new people to the detail, to ensure everything runs smoothly,' Roy Jones, the security boss said.

'I will be taking over the job my husband had. We will have regular meetings, so please help me learn the ropes. Don't hesitate to correctmy mistakes. We have a tough job ahead of us,' Rebecca Carpo stated.

64

CHAPTER TWENTY-TWO

Anthony's mother was so adamant in her demands that there wouldbe no connection between her youngest son and her husband's business, she had given him her maiden last name- Smithe. She understood why the young man kept the last request of the Don from her, but it almost ruined both their lives.

Anthony began his final year of school. The plans were for him to turn pro and compete on the PGA Tour. Yet first, He had to deal with the turmoil in his mind concerning Susan Smith. Here were twopeople with similar names, given to them by their parents, differentfrom the family names. Both because of their fathers' notoriety. Strange coincidence, he pondered. Along with the fact they both loved the game of golf. A game which brought them together, but at the same time was keeping them apart.

Susan was at the moment, deep in thought about this very same person. She knew their paths were bound to cross again. 'How am Igoing to handle this?' she pondered.

Dad, have you heard anything from Anthony and his mother', Susan asked.

'Yes, Susan, I have, and it is good news. Mrs. Carpo will keep the casino and run the operation herself. Anthony will finish his schooling and turn pro next year. Have you figured out how you are going to react to seeing him again? There will be a lot of interest from the newsmedia concerning you two kids, he said.

'I know, and also because of you, Dad. There will not be any contact other than normal greetings. Maybe, down the road, there could come a time when I can put aside what he had promised his father, she said.

'Don't base your evaluation of Tony on his promise to his dad. It was somuch easier to agree with a man who is about to die than to deny his last request, Sue. His mistake was not telling his mother, I think,' Jack said.

Well, I'll let things happen as they happen. What about you, Dad?Do you plan on entering any tournament, or are your serious golf-playing days behind you, old man', she joked?

'I'm glad you asked, young lady. I will begin earnest preparations shortly to qualify for this year's American Open. My exemptions have expired, so I've got to start all over, going through the grind, he said.

'Great, Dad. We will commence practice starting tomorrow. The guys have our little course in good condition, Susan said.

CHAPTER TWENTY-THREE

Jack had assembled everyone together in the 'big room', as he called the spacious area where the large television was. All of his families, along with the Smith and Jordan clans, were there.

'We have been anxious to hear your plans concerning our living arrangements', Sam Jordan spoke up.

'As you know, we have completed work on our new village. It is ready for us to move in. I've asked for this meeting to announce what I propose we do about the use of the place. I believe we are still in danger from the mob, especially since Anthony's mother has decided to personally operate her casino. She refuses to sell out to the mob, and there is no telling how her move is going to play out,' Jack said.

'How does her move affect our families?' Bette Smith asked. 'There is no connection between us other than past events which seem to be settled. Do you think we will have to worry about them for the rest of our lives?

Everyone was focused on Jack Proctor. After investing a substantial amount of money in the 'Town Ranch', it was evident to everyone that his motivations extended beyond simply relocating from the pleasant place they had all resided in for an extended period.

'I want to offer up a plan of action pertaining to Mrs. Carpo's casino. She is going to take on a job with no experience, without the main people who were the operational force at the place. I believe she will run into big problems, even though the guys from New York leave her alone. She will require assistance in both financial and management aspects. I want to get involved in Vegas. We need a business to focus our future on. If matters develop the way I believe they will, this casino seems perfect. Here is how I propose we get involved,' he said.

'First, I want you to promise you will voice your opinion on my plan. Reject it, modify it. Please help me with this matter, folks. I feel a need to help the lady if I can. However, you must make a choice of your own as to our actions, he said.

CHAPTER TWENTY-FOUR

'I am convinced we have about one year before my plan will be needed. We will use the time to start getting ready for possible conflict with the New York mob. First, we will move but will not desert this place. I believe those guys already know all about thislocation, so we will use some of our security guards as if they are ourfamilies still living here. Most of the people will move with us, leavingenough to convince the world everything is the same. This will be thecrux of our defense. Allow them to enter and then encircle them, creating a trap between the fortified and armed structures here. he said.

'Why do you think they will come after us? They know the FBI ison our side. I would believe they fear the G-men enough not to tacklethem,' Susan spoke up.

'Yeah, Jack, I don't think they want us that bad,' Sam Jordan said. 'This is all about possibilities, folks. We must be prepared for every

action they can take against us. I mentioned we have about a year. The casino will probably be in trouble pretty soon but should avoid drastic steps, such as bankruptcy or seeking loans, until then. Whenthis happens, I want us to step in and bail the lady out, he said. Now,here is my plan.

CHAPTER TWENTY-FIVE

'All the adults here will start learning how to operate a gambling casino from the ground up. We will do it through the Internetand visits to places everywhere except Vegas. Online courses, and finding the ins and outs of the business, Jack said.

'When the time comes Mrs. Carpo seeks either financing, or a buyer, I want us to come forward with an offer to be her partner. Witha managing team and over 400 million dollars. I want to have 49% of the company for two years. If, afterwards, she wants to continue the arrangement, buy us out, or sell us the whole place, the choice wouldbe hers. We would run the place until then, he said.

'What about our golf plans, Dad?

'You will be in school when I begin qualifying for the U.S. Open.I want you to keep your mind on what happens to you, young lady. IfI make it, then we can begin thinking about me. Something tells methere is going to be a big distraction coming your way. I cannot believeAndy will be able to stay away from you very long, Susan. This is goingto be a very busy year for all of us, Jack Proctor said.

'Dad, I want to caddy for you in both events. School will be overwhen the Open begins, so it will be only a few days for me to take leave,so I can carry your bag during your qualification rounds,' Susan said.

Jack listened to his young daughter being so grown-up. Her offer to caddy for him brought a smile to his face. He knew it would not be very long before she would be leaving the nest, and his 'daddy' feelings were getting to him. It was a nice thought he had to remind him she would always be his daughter, just not his 'little girl'.

'Okay, young lady. Your wish is my command,' he replied.

CHAPTER TWENTY-SIX

Anthony was not pleased by his mother's decision to keep and run the casino. He did not believe she had the experience necessary to undertake such a significant job. Plus, the whole business reminded him of the life he lived under his father's career. It was not a happy place at home, as he was in constant conflict with everyone but his mother.

'I know you are doing this for both of us, Mother. Isn't there another way you can enjoy growing old without feeling you have to worry about my future? I am fine with the love and devotion you have always shown me. You do not have to prove anything. It really bothers me how you have loaded yourself with work and problems,' Andy said.

'I need to do this, young man. Not for you, but to keep busy with a useful project. I don't want to be alone anymore. There are a lot of fine people looking to me for their livelihood, and we will succeed. This is for me, Anthony,' she said.

CHAPTER TWENTY-SEVEN

The first phase of the qualifying went fine. Jack scored well enoughto advance to the final rounds. 'This is the real test, Susan. Thereare a lot of tour pros competing for only a few openings, and most of them made it to this phase. I know you have read where Andy is also trying to qualify. He will join our group tomorrow. It sure wouldbe ironic for us to play together, huh, dear,' Jack said.

Susie found out yesterday what her dad was talking about. The fun time of the first round was a thing of the past. Now, she was faced with conflicting emotions. Both Jack and Anthony were very unlikely to secure spots in the Open. Only two places were available in this segment, with a load of good players in the field. She hated to think of either not making the big show, but it was certainly going to be a long shot for either of them to win a spot. There was a very good chance neither would survive.

'Gee, Dad. How come fate has thrown us together again under these conditions? It will be nice to see the guy, but what a deal,' she said.

'I have a feeling golf is going to take a back seat when you two see each other again, Susan. Try not to take sides and let us enjoy the competition. We are going to be swamped by the media because everyone expects Anthony and me to be in the mix. Both of us played really well to reach this final round,' Jack said.

'I don't know how our meeting again is going to play out, Dad. It is hard to get over the shock I felt when all this about his family came to light. Has he tried to contact me?' she said.

'I don't know, Suzie. Our phone is strictly private, and our address doesn't register anywhere. Did your paths not cross this past golf season, Jack asked.

'No, we were never even close. I guess he thinks I hold a grudge against him, or else he could have dropped a note for me at the school', she said.

CHAPTER TWENTY-EIGHT

Anthony had kept up with Jack's progress. Susan and her dadwere on the news every day. The reporters were constantly asking him about their relationship, to the point of it being annoying. How many times can you tell them there is no relationship, he thought. He knew the annoyance came from the painful admission that he very much wanted to be a part of Susan's life. He saw the tee-time schedule and knew he would be three foursomes behind Jack's group. Far enough apart, yet oh, so close, he thought. How am I going to handle this, he pondered?

Jack had been on the practice tee for some time when Anthony moved toward his assigned spot. Susan saw him approach and nudged her father. They spotted each other at about the same time.

All eyes in the practice area were focused on the upcoming meeting. Anthony extended his hand to Jack, and they exchanged greetings. He turned to Susan with the same gesture, but she walked toward the young man and took him in her arms in a loose embrace, putting the guy in astate of shock.

She stepped back, holding his hand, looked him in the eyes, and said, 'Hello, Tony. I've missed you!

Anthony felt the load of the world had been lifted from his shoulders. The anxiety that had built up in him about this encounter flew out the window because of the warm greeting this lovely woman had just given him.

'I've missed you too, Susan. Please meet me afterwards for a snack in the dining hall. Right now, I've got to find a golf game you just made me lose, or I am going to be eaten alive by your dad on the course', he said.

CHAPTER TWENTY-NEINE

'Dad, this is turning into a good round of golf. You keep hitting shots like this approach, and we are going to the Open', Susansaid.

'I'm feeling really confidant, Susie. We are currently positioned near the top; however, the remaining holes will present significant challenges. You know, I can remember every hole I played over twenty years ago. I had to constantly remind myself to staycalm and trust my swing. The old swagger is coming back. We are goingto make the cut, young lady, he said.

True to his word, they ended up one shot in the lead. Anthony was two strokes behind, placing him in third place. There was a mob ofmedia surrounding them, each pushing cameras and mikes in their faces, as they finished. Everyone wanted to see and report on this event.

'Anthony will be in the twosome just ahead of us. This final round is going to be fun. Great golf, and the nation looking for signs of a love affair, Suzan, Jack said.

'Daddy, there is not a love affair,' she said.

'Maybe not, young lady. However, you might call it an affectionate, mutual attraction, huh? It is quite obvious the folks will be looking for a little more than a golf tournament tomorrow, which is going toramp up the pressure. Do you want me to consider getting someoneelse to carry my bag? It might help Anthony, he said.

'No, I am going to meet him in a few minutes in the dining room.I'll put his mind at ease about us so he can concentrate on his game.Thanks for the offer, though. You are a good man, Dad. We will havefun,' she said.

CHAPTER THIRTY

Mrs. Carpo was headed home after a long day at the casino. Herhabit was to have a drink while watching the evening news.

Tonight, she skipped the ritual and went right to bed. She roseup the next morning, refreshed, as she brought her coffee into the sittingroom and turned on the television. There, on the screen, was a picture ofher son being hugged by a young woman.

Holy Mac, she thought. What is going on? Then, she recognized the lady. The announcer explained that the encounter happened at the U. S. Open qualifying event. Mr. Jack Proctor and his daughter were being greeted by Anthony Smithe in the practice area. The event had been anticipated by the media and the many golf fans around the world.

'We all knew of the connection between Anthony and Jack sincethe details of the famous wager became known. Everyone was lookingto see the reaction of the two men as they met. However, everythingabout the matter was swept aside by Susan's warm embrace of a startled young man, the television announcer said.

Anthony's mother observed the event as it occurred yesterday.The first round of the qualifying finals was completed with Jack andAnthony two shots apart. Tony had the lead on a final birdie. It was 18holes of golf, and the two men dominated, leaving them with a good lead over the field.

'I'm glad to see Tony playing so well. He had a lot of pressure on his game today. He will do quite well on the tour,' Jack said.

'Me, too. You didn't do so bad, Old Man. Except for missing those two putts, you would be in the lead. It crossed my mind you were not unhappy about the results. Am I wrong, Dad?' Susan asked.

'I believe Tony is a better golfer when he is in the lead. Some people play their best from the front. It is a good trait if managed correctly.Tony seems to be mentally prepared to win,' he said

Jack was not going to admit he purposely missed those putts. They were both over 20 feet, so making them would have been very good. However, he was playing to get a spot in the Open, not to win the qualifying rounds. He was far enough ahead of the pack to be safe in making pars. After watching Tony all day, he felt certain the two ofthem would secure the two places up for grabs. Tomorrow will be the final round, and they will play together in the last group.

I am going to help Anthony as much as possible, Susan. Being together will really give me a chance to make sure he stays in the lead. I have always taught you to manage your own game while keeping your eyes on the opposition. I can't talk to the other players, but you can. There is something I want you to pass on to the guy. He is prone to one mistake in his swing, and this is it,' he said.

Jack taped several of Anthony's swings today. Susan picked up on what Tony was doing. It was a tendency easy to correct if caughtbefore it was ingrained in the swing. He wanted her to saunter over towhere Anthony would be warming up and point out to his caddy what was developing.

'Make sure you tell the caddy you want Anthony to advance intothe Open. He might think you were attempting to mess with his head. If he is a good caddy, he will pass it on. You will get another chanceduring the round to mention it again if he does not, Jack said.

CHAPTER THIRTY-ONE

It was an excellent round of golf for both players. The crowd following them grew at every hole and became very vocal after each shot. This seemed to spur Anthony, and he responded with enthusiasm. Jack knew it helped, but he knew the guy was also showingoff in front of Susan. The young lady played her part, reacting happilywhen he made a good shot. The result was a first-place finish and aninvite to the big dance. Jack stayed within a couple of strokes all day and was second in the standings.

The young couple was seated at a corner table in the dining area, unsuccessfully attempting to avoid all the media and fans filling the room. By facing the windows overlooking the putting surface, they could talk without the throng lip-reading their conversation.

'My caddy just told me about the tip you gave him concerning my swing flaw. Why did you do it, Susan? It made the difference in our scores today,' he asked.

'Dad asked me to tell you, Tony. He picked up on it yesterday. Ithink he wanted you to end up on top. Above all else, he is really a teacher at heart. He spent many hours with my sister and me as we began learning the game. When he saw your problem, he couldn't resisthelping you get rid of it. Plus, he really wants you to succeed. We will have fun at the Open, win or lose. Dad has a master's in his sightsnext year. He has to finish as the top amateur in the field to get a spot, although I think the top ten places get an invite. Since you are turning pro, he won't try to beat you. Isn't it nice of him to give you such abreak, she said.

Anthony was ready to move to a new level with this beautiful lady,but he could tell she was not. He respected her feelings and kept the talklight and friendly, while his heart was screaming Love you, Susan. Hiseyes left no doubt as to how he felt about her, and Susan was well awareof the attraction between them. Both were young, and she was not going

to rush into any type of relationship. It would have to weather the time
needed to grow into anything deeper. She could not afford to let himknow
her true feelings. The 'woman mystic' would be his farefor the near future.

CHAPTER THIRTY-TWO

The casino should be doing better, profit-wise. The overheadhas not gone up, and the play is about the same. We could tighten up the slots, but then we lose our reputation as the best in town in that department. We may be running into a period of badluck, so let's keep our eyes open for card-counters, especially. I know you are all on high alert, and I thank you for doing such a good job,Mrs. Carpo said.

She was holding a special meeting with the pit bosses and Security. They were aware of her concern, as her anxiety was easy to see. It was well known to them all about their cash reserve situation. If they continued to see big winners at the tables, matters could really go south.

'Word gets around pretty fast in this town, which houses are offering the best returns. This might turn into a positive with increased play. It could go the other way, too. I don't want this to leave the room, but Iam going to instruct our lawyer to discreetly discuss ways to infuse some capital into the business. I tell you this, folks, to reassure everyone we will survive. Be careful not to let our worries be known. The wolves are out there, and you know who I mean, the Boss said.

CHAPTER THIRTY-THRE

The day of the beginning of the U.S. Open golf tournament has arrived. In most media comments, the story is that this tournamentwill be the best in many years. An American is listed as number one in the world. He is followed closely by a European player, both at thetop of their game. Added to the mix is the saga of the Proctor drama. There is always a whole lot of hype connected to the 'Open', with fullmedia coverage. Plus, there is the possibility that someone among the goodgolfers will get hot.

The romance between Susan and Anthony had really blossomed into a love affair. Jack had given his daughter the 'Okay' to tag along withher lover's group instead of being his caddy, but she wanted to stay withhim. She was receiving a lot of attention from young men. Several were persistent young professional golfers, but there was a special attraction toward Anthony, and she knew he cared for her. It was easy for her to separate the 'lust' attention from the 'love' attraction Anthony showered on her. He was so open about his feelings; it made it impossible for her not to return his admiration.

'I am glad you are with me, Susan. You are a great assistant to me, as well as a 'bagger.' I worried you might be a distraction to Anthony if he could see you up close as he made his shots. So much of this game is in the head as well as in the hand. I want to see him do well in this event,' Jack Proctor said.

'Come on, Dad. Don't talk like you are not planning on being the winner. To heck with any loser thoughts. We are the best pair in the field, for sure,' she said.

I'm not talking as much about my play as I am about Anthony's. He is more afront runner, which has a downside. He needs to learn how to come frombehind. Several of these guys are sure to put on a show and shoot 'lights out'in any round. I feel pretty sure what my score will be, give or take a couple of shots. It depends on the putter. Let's hope we both do well,' he said.

CHAPTER THIRTY-FOUR

The day of the tournament was at hand, with all the hoopla coming headlong at all the players. Jack watched Tony as he was warming up on the practice tee. Susan was also doing the same.

'He is doing fine. Not rushing things, as the guy next to him is. See the fast turn on the downswing? His caddy is not watching him closely enough. Take note, young lady. Your job is very important. More than looking verypretty and totting a bag. I really am only joking with you. Just remindingmyself to stay loose is what I am actually doing,' Jack said.

'I hear you, Pops. This is beginning to get to me, though. All the cameras and reporters sticking mikes in your face have got to have Anthony hyped up. I try to smile broadly whenever he looks my way,but I'm closing it down right now. He got a little careless with a couple of shots. Stay focused, dear, she whispered.

CHAPTER THIRTY-FIVE

Jack saw the tournament begin to play out just as he envisioned. The more seasoned pros were getting the feel for the layout, playing it close to the vest. The newcomers were all over the course, except Anthony. He was quite a few twosomes ahead of himand Susan, but they were keeping up with him by watching the leader board.

'He is really playing well. He just came through several tough holes in fine shape. We are both torn between our own game and how Tony is faring. It is not a distraction, but I am going to have to stay well-focused from here on. We will catch up on his progress at the turn, Jack said.

On the one hand, Anthony felt glad Susan was not close by. Her presence would have been nice, but she overpowered him. Yet here he was, playingliterally alone. Not a single familiar face in the few people around his group. An unknown golfer with no friends to cheer him on. He looked back toward the fairway where Jack and Susan were playing. He could make out the group following them, and it was large. He heard the sound as Jack hit his ball. His stride told everyone he was proud of the results.

In the middle of a contest in a premier golf tournament held inthe USA, Tony was daydreaming.

'Hey, where are you, man? It is your shot,' his caddy said.

'I was watching someone else, Buddy. It will not happen again. I want to win very much. Let's go get them, Tony said.

CHAPTER THIRTY-SIX

Which was almost what the young man did. He played a wonderful four-round tournament, coming within one stroke of winning the US Open. He lost to an eagle on the last hole, as a ball hit the flag, got wrapped up in it, and dropped right into thecup. As Jack approached the last hole, he was more interested in Tony than he was because of the fact he was two strokes behind and putting for a par. He was happy about his results but knew Anthony felt robbed of winning. Susan put her arm around him, offering comfort as best she could.

'It's the golf gods, Tony. They just sprung a new one on you. There will be nothing on the news but the guy's shot- heard round the world. It does not take away from a great tournament you played in. The British Open awaits you, young man. Go get 'em, Jack said.

CHAPTER THIRTY-SEVEN

Jack had important business to attend to. His finish in the US Open got him an invite to the Masters next spring, and it waswhat he was gunning for. He had set up a meeting with Mrs. Carpo at her casino. This would be attended by him and his group from the ranch, so he had to put golf on the back burner right now. Awhole lot of people's futures were riding on the outcome of this confab, for sure.

'I called us all together to present a proposal, Mrs. Carpo. We have been aware of your problems here all along. I have had my people draw up a whole lot of plans we want to present to you to solve each andevery one of them. First, let us recognize the distinct possibility of our families being joined in a small way. Our daughter and your son arevery much in love. We will not be surprised or disappointed if they aremarried. In fact, it would be wonderful. We do admire Anthony very much. This has little to do with what I am about to offer, but it doesmake it easier to talk together, don't you think?', Jack said.

'Our group is prepared to put about 500 million dollars, plus a large piece of real estate to be named later, and a construction loan large enough to build a first-class casino to replace yours. We will ask for 49 percent interest in your business for two years. At the endof this time, you will have complete control of one of three options.First, revert back and pay us off. Second, give us the option to buy youout. Third, to continue the agreement we make today. If youare receptive to our offer, we will proceed with all the details. If youare not, we stop right now', Jack said.

The look of shock she knew was plastered on her face was nothing to what she was feeling inside. This morning, she realized the days of her beloved casino were numbered. Not enough money and no realistic prospects for a bail-out. Now, out of the blue, she was being offered everything she needed. It overwhelmed her, and she burst into tears. Then

This gang of people began to clap and laugh instead of acting sorry forher sobs. They rushed to hug and pat her on the back. Everyone had taken her reaction as a 'yes' to Jack's offer. They had nailed it, for sure.

I accept your offer, but it seems everyone already knows what I plan to do, huh', she said.

CHAPTER THIRTY-EIGHT

'We will go over the details later. Right now, I have something to show you. This is a video of your corridor where your people take the cash boxes from the floor to the counting room in the basement. Four guys escort a cart to the elevator and down to the vault. You do these four times a day, right? Notice the bend in the hallway about halfway through. Also, notice the only door, right at the bend. There is no knob, so it cannot be opened from the hall. This door opens to the electrician's workroom. They use it to gain access to the casino and is never opened otherwise, Jack said.

'Mrs. Carpo, you have been subjected to 'skimming' for a long time. My operatives found out how it was being pulled off. The electricians had placed cameras in the hall, leaving a small blank coverage in front of the electrician's door. One of the identical carts was rolled out of the room and placed in the center of the hall by one man. The cart from the casino would run right up to and butt against the second one, nudging it forward. The four men would quickly slide forward and continue down the hall with the new cart. The electrician would take the first cart into the room, he said.

'By watching monitors on each game table, the electricians knew how much money was in each box. They would fill their boxes with an amount less than what was taken from the original boxes. Each box produced a percent of the take, enabling them to 'skim' a certain amount of money each trip each day. If the table was very active, more would come from its box than a table less used. Everything was managed by the eight men on the carts and eight electricians. The cart men would make a run at the start of their shifts, and the end, which meant there was an eight-hour shift in the middle with no one on duty. One electrician was assigned to take the money out the door from their room to the outside of the casino. No one inspected their cozy workshop. The beauty of it all was they would skip the transfer if anyone else was close by, Jack said.

'I have taken these men and their families to a safe place, wherethey are being questioned very thoroughly. Everything is to be recordedand handled professionally. They are employed by the same mob familywho wanted to take over your business, Mrs. Carpo. We are not going to the FBI. If we turn this over to the authorities, all hell will break loose. They will halt operations here while they investigate. You couldeven lose your license or at least have it suspended. And you will not get the money you lost. It will be gone. Plus, you may have to pay allback taxes and levies owed on the money stolen, plus penalties. Here ismy plan to avert all this happening,' he said.

'There are two of the guys involved who are 'made' men in the family. The others were just soldiers. We will get complete confessions from everyone, and it will all be taped. We will send copies along with oneof the inside men to the head 'Don' of all the mob in New York City. The man will be instructed to talk only to the heads of each family in a one-time setting. The FBI may have an 'insider' planted, and we must not let any of this be known. If it does become known, all avenues opened to us will be closed. We take everything to the media if it gets out. The number one 'Don' will be given the figure of how much money was skimmed. We will ask him to replace what was stolen in exchange for forgetting the matter. Otherwise, we turn everything over to the FBI, Jack said.

CHAPTER THIRTY-NINE

Everyone was quick to see how Jack's plan should be accepted by the bosses in New York. The Feds would blame all the familiesand come after everyone. The group that initiated this event never shared it with anyone else. They also went against orders to stay outof the casinos. All the men, except the 'made' ones, would be given an opportunity to live at the village ranch. Along with their families, theplace would become everyone's 'safe haven'.

'We will know soon enough how it will go down. In the meantime, we will proceed with plans to modernize the casino, Jack said.

'How will changes to the building help us attract more customers?The new area for most of the action is not on the 'strip' where we arenow. I cannot see how spending money on our location will cure ourlack of new players, Mrs. Carpo said.

'I have an 'ace' up my sleeve, folks. I mentioned a large piece ofreal estate. On my second visit here, when I was setting up my bet Iran across a 500- acre plot of desert for sale. It was truly a desolatepatch several miles from the city limits. I bought it under my father'scompany name. Over the years, I have built a golf course and clubhouse. I brought irrigation there, and you will recognize it as the lush'Texas Land Grant.' I named it years ago in honor of my parents. Dad always referred to our home as such. Right now, it sits close to the new batch of super casinos, which have moved outward toward the property. The course is built into the desert landscape, with very fewfairways. I have maintained the environment by spotting landing areas between the holes. It is a championship course. With Anthony as thehead professional and my teaching school there, we will apply for aspot on the PGA Tour. Here are the plans we drew up showing the casino and the motel with many small cabins located throughout theproperty, Jack said.

'So, you own the most talked-about piece of real estate in this partof the state. I read several months ago that a group was offering millions tobuy the place,' a pit boss named Sam said.

'Mr. Proctor, this information certainly makes your proposal a very lucrative offer. It is true you never have had any gambling device on your place? I know it is zoned and licensed for a casino. How did you foresee the city growing in your direction', Mrs. Carpo asked?

'My people secured all of the papers and got them renewed every year. It was done as an insurance policy in case I decided to add gambling. I have received many offers over the years. It has become almost a weekly occurrence lately. I would never have sold it, regardless of the offer. It is my family's memorial, if you will. Adding the casino will complete the honor. I had no problem securing the necessary finances for buildingour project because of this hunk of land. I could see this was the onlydirection the city could grow. It motivated me to buy the place. We willbe on the edge of the best spot in town,' Jack said.

'You met the boss of the construction company I hope to place the building contract with. This will happen with your approval, but he has come up with a two-year time frame for completion. He has worked closely with the architectural firm. They are available to you, Mrs. Carpo. This is your baby, so put your stamp on it,' Jack said.

CHAPTER FORTY

The man Jack sent to New York had returned. He had not beentold of the plans Jack had to shelter anyone who wanted it. Thestress of his journey and the fear for the safety of his family weighed heavily on the guy. The fact that the main man had accepted thedeal made it even worse. He knew someone was going to pay for this caper. He just hoped all the wrath would go toward the guilty familyand this outfit out here. Realism told him all these men involved wouldsuffer in some way unless they went into hiding. However, he was sickfrom worrying as he approached Jack Proctor.

'The Don has agreed to your terms. The money will be passed as you requested, the mobster said.

'You did a good job. All the families of your friends and you will be offered a new life if you want it. Anyone desiring to return to their old employers is free to leave with no strings attached. Those who stay will be treated like the FBI does under their 'witness protectionprogram. No details will be offered until everyone makes up their minds. Each family will be isolated until they choose. We do not want those returning to have any idea what will happen to those who stay.You go first. Go greet your family in the next room. Take your time.This is serious business, as you well know,' Jack said.

Everyone agreed to put their past associations with the mob behind them and accept Jack's offer of a safe haven. No one had dreamed their years of criminal activities at the casino would be forgiven in this manner. The wives and children had never been told their men were involved in unlawful employment, although the families knew not toever discuss their work.

'I am glad we were not told about the work our guys were doing. Did anyone really know what was going on', Tony's mother said.

'Sam told me he became very worried when Mrs. Carpo refused to sell her business. He warned me never to ask or talk about his work.You can tell all the men are relieved but worried about our future, especially the children's welfare. Mr. Proctor has assured us of the precautions taken for our safety,' another wife said.

CHAPTER FORTY-ONE

Jack had gotten all the people in his original group together for a meeting. He did not include the casino families. The fewer in onhis plans, the better, was how he summarized the get-together.

'We have the families from the casino scam headed for our new home. With the security we have in place, everyone will be safe there. All of our neighbors are well-established, large ranches stretching for many miles in each direction. Visitors stand out like a sore thumb and seldom hang around when they realize how desolate the area is, Jack said.

'Several of those ranchers have come into our town and shoppedin the stores. I know they came by more out of curiosity than a desire to buy. They all were full of questions about our nice little town springing up in their midst. Our cover story of reopening the mineis perfect,' Sam Jordan said.

'With the arrival of these casino folks, we will have a nice community along the road to our ranch house. Add the security forces and their families, and it will be a normal village for the kids to grow up in. I want to stress the importance of this because we are going to be inviting a confrontation with the mob in New York. We need to bring an end tothis whole business with those folks, and this is my plan, Jack said.

He outlined his intentions of offering their old ranch as bait to themob if they had plans to avenge the losses they had just incurred. Jack felt sure a deep resentment existed toward him. Big and deep enough tocome after him if an opportunity opened for them to act on. To the outside world, everyone would still be living as before, along with the families from the casino, except the security forces. They would seem to have been withdrawn.

'I want to present a scene portraying a defenseless, peaceful home, free of any anxiety about their safety. Those folks will commit an act of revenge if they feel such a move can be made without proof against them. A lightning strike as a payback is their modus operandi. Weare going to offer them their chance. I believe the mob in New Yorkis united under the leadership of one man. They were all in on the scheme against Mrs. Carpo. Otherwise, there would have been a warover one family's defiance of an agreement to stay out of gamblinghere. It is just too tempting for them to pass over the chance to get afoothold in this business, he said.

'Will this move impact the work on the new casino, Jack? Couldn't it wait until after we complete everything', Mrs. Jordan asked.

'Now seems to be the ideal time to test the mob's intentions toward us. Plus, we should not live under such a threat any longer. Enoughis enough. I may be wrong about their goals. I hope so, but let's findout, folks. Our security company has been working hard to infiltrateone of the families in New York. I wanted to find out the habits of the super Don. We have come up with a plan to kidnap him and hisimmediate family if he strikes against us. This work has been going onfor some time, folks, and it is paying off. I want those people to knowwe have the means to really hurt them and will not play by their rulesof separation when it comes to their next of kin. They attack all of us,we do the same to them. Everything is set, except getting the word out about our complacency. Our guys back east are on it right now, Jacksaid.

CHAPTER FORTY-TWO

The work on the new casino was in full swing. The news of theirplans spread throughout the gambling world, which seemedto have spurred tourism in their town, along with the play at the gambling houses. This was according to most of the businesses along the strip. With the addition to the ownership and the location,property around the 'Texas Land Grant' became hot real estate. They had about two years of construction in front of them before movingday, but it felt like the right time for Jack to initiate the rest of his plan against the mob.

Jack had called a construction meeting in the casino conference room. There were a few details to work out, but everything was proceeding on schedule. While this was important business, he could tell most of the people associated with his family were uneasy. As he closed the discussion, he requested those folks to stay for further news.

'I can see you guys are really nervous, so I am going to give you something to cheer you up. There is another part of my plans concerning our friends in New York. The last thing I want is to have a heated confrontation with those thugs, and I know you all feel the same way.I told you how we were going to take the number one Don and hisfamily. Well, our people came up with the idea to go after one of thelesser families first. We have done just such a thing, folks. Yesterday we returned the ones who originated the skim operation after two days of captivity. During the ordeal, they were completely isolated, never seeing or hearing anything. We released them on the estate of the big guy in the middle of the night. All cloak and dagger stuff, right out of a gangster movie. The warning was further amplified when a note addressed to the super Don was found on the pillow of a child of another family. It read: Yours is next. Some of our operatives are past CIA and FBI guys. They know their stuff, Jack said.

The relief was quite evident on the haggard faces of all in attendance. They were only now getting used to the presence of the former mobsters and their families. They were well-liked but quite subdued by all the changes to their lifestyles. Jack was very pleased with the way his people had welcomed them. They were all big city folks who missed the bright lights and urban living. He constantly reminded them that what was happening could be only a temporary moment in their lives.

'We are working hard to find jobs for all of you who want to go back to your past careers. Not in the casinos, but where we can match yourskills in other areas. Stay cool and enjoy the moment, guys, he said.

CHAPTER FORTY-THREE

Jack was ready to move on to the next major event in his life. The Masters golf tournament was about six months away, and he had a big job awaiting him. He moved to the new ranch and had his people at work building a replica of what he had inthe way of golf at the old place. All the latest digital equipment to record his workouts was being installed. He needed instant play the back of his swing, stance, and flight path of the balls he struck. He was embarking on an entirely new phase of his life as he trainedfor this much-anticipated event. He taught himself how to play the game with help from his dad, so working alone without professional help kept his workouts to himself. The refinements he would be introducing to his game were garnered through films and books of the famous heroes of the sport. His goal was to refine everything asbest he could and spring a surprise on the golf world.

The day began with filming several hours of ball-striking, followed by many more in study and analysis. He knew every facet of his game had to be deeply embedded in his muscle memory, with no need to think about how he was moving. This was going beyond anything he hadever done, and it began to pay off as the days and weeks went by.

CHAPTER FORTY-FOUR

Jim Carraige was at his desk, fast at work, wrapping up the finaldetails of the early edition of his paper. The job as the head mancame with a lot of headaches. Since becoming editor-in-chief three years ago, he had made a name for himself in the industry. It hadbeen a long journey from his cub reporter days, and he had just beenbuzzed by his secretary the 'man was on the phone. The guy who hadhelped propel his career, Jack Proctor, was calling. How ironic thathe had justfinished an editorial on the upcoming Master's tournament, set to be inprint next week. He never lost interest in the story generated all thoseyears ago and was still writing about it every year.

'I want to invite you to an exclusive interview with me right after the last round, Mr. Carraige. I have several big announcements to make, regardless of whether I win or not. Can you make it? I know the job kept you from following me at the Open, but I read your article reminding people of our past history. I know it will be well worth your time, Jack Proctor said.

CHAPTER FORTY-FIVE

The day of the tournament had arrived. Most of the media and people associated with the event felt Jack Proctor's presence had ramped up the public interest this year. He was not regarded as one of the top players, but his past success in the major events made him the crowd favorite. Plus, there was the romantic tie to Anthony Smithe. Susan would be her father's caddy, and there were many chances the two young folks could interact during the four days of the meet. The word was they were a 'couple', which added fuel to the fire of speculation making the rounds. It was all business, though, as Jack and his daughter entered the first tee box. They had come directly from the parking lot, bypassing the practice area. No one ever started their round of golf without warming up. The crowd was in shock when that happened, but it was soon replaced by awe and wonder at the brilliant play and score posted in the first five holes by Jack Proctor. He was six under, with birdies on four holes and an eagle on number two. He finished the front nine with two more birdies, for an eight under par score.

'We have just seen a perfect display of golf. I am shocked at watching this man play. It is remarkable because this is not the swing Jack had at the U.S. Open last year. Something is different, but I can't pick it out,' the expert in the booth stated.

The discussion was cut short when Jack drove his ball at the start of the back nine. A perfect shot, followed by another within two feet of the flag. He entered what is known as 'Amen Corner' nine under par and emerged with one par, one birdie, and one eagle. With five holes to play, he needed one more sub-par birdie to possibly shoot a 59 at the Masters tournament. He got it on the par 5 sixteenth and added another on the last hole for a score of 14 under par 58.

CHAPTER FORTY-SIX

Jack was surrounded by cameras, microphones, and cell phones as he and Susan came out of the official scorer's tent. After posing for everyone, he announced he would not be discussing today's round.

'I am going to let the media coverage of my golf score be your source of information, folks. We have three more days of play, and anything can happen. I have never been one with any desire to talk about a tournament until it is over, so I will see you tomorrow,' Jack said.

CHAPTER FORTY-SEVEN

The second day of the Masters began under ideal weather conditions. There was very little wind, with plenty of Georgia sunshine. Susan walked a few holes to get the feel of the greens and fairways. They were in the same degree of firmness on the putting surfaces, with the change of hole placements usually used for later rounds.

'They have toughened the course, Dad. Your score has gotten their attention. Maybe they don't want any more like yesterday, but this is going to make it difficult for anyone to catch you,' Susan said.

'I expected they would follow such a low score round by making it harder to have another birdie-binge, as some are calling my play. Actually, this should make my job easier. We will see. Let's tee it up, young lady,' Jack said.

They finished the day with an eight under 64, leaving him with a total of 22 under par. He followed with a third round 66 and a fourth day 65, for a tournament record 253.

'I am going to have a closed one-on-one interview right now with Jim Carraige. He will have complete control of the contents of our sit-down. Mr. Carraige started covering my golf career from the beginning, and I owe him this exclusive, Jack said.

CHAPTER FORTY-EIGHT

They were seated in a conference room with only cameras and recording equipment. Jack wanted complete isolation for this session as he had important things to talk about.

'I have three announcements to discuss with you, Mr. Carraige. The first is to tell you this is my last competitive round of golf. My last revelation will explain this one fully.

I have a story to tell you about the tournament we just finished and how I was able to have the remarkable results of these past four days of golf. Here goes:

Everything I have done this past year was for the sole purpose of playing in this Masters event. After I secured my invite by where I finished in the

U.S. Open. I went into training six months ago. The method of workouts I used came to me through two sources. The first was a book written by a famous golfer named Ben Hogan. I think it was published sometime in the 1950s. Mr. Hogan revealed at the time his use of a feature in the golf swing called the 'pronation of the wrists' maneuver during the beginning of the swing. It was a slight rotation of the wrists at the start of the take-away. The accepted way to start the action is to have the wrists remain inactive until the cocking at the top of the swing. Mr. Hogan's use of this 'amateurish' move resulted in a higher arch in the trajectory of the ball and in a softer landing. He stated he used this only about 20% of the time, or when this type of shot was needed. I used the term that some of Mr. Hogan's fellow competitors called his innovation. It was dismissed by them as 'foolish'. Years later, I read about another great golfer, Lee Trevino's announcement that he would not play in the Masters because the course required a high arch shot, while his flight path was low.

He would hit a perfect approach shot and watch it roll through the green.

'I began to put the two stories together. Mr. Hogan suffered a car accident, resulting in bad leg injuries. This limited his play to only the major events, which the Masters certainly qualified. Was the innovation in his swing directed toward the course Mr. Trevino described? I started working on the duplication of his maneuver and found another change in my swing made the ball strike even better,' he said.

'Most modern-day golf swings are pretty much the same, however, there is one aspect where there is a lot of variances, and this is in the grip of the club. There is the full finger, interlock, overlap, plus different use of pressure points in the hands. Along with how the hands are placed on the shaft, which indicated what is called either a weak or strong grip. I found the correct use of my hands when using Mr. Hogan's discovery. How I added this element will remain my secret. The results of six months of practice and experiment were displayed in my play in this tournament.

'Now here is where you come into the picture, Mr. Carraige. I am going to open a golf school at the location where our new casino is being built. The name will be 'James Carraige Golf Academy'. It will be an invitation-only, free school for young golfers from all over the world. I will invite those whom I deem to have the promised desire and talent to succeed at the upper levels of the game. It will be offered free, along with room and board, as long as the student progresses. Either the golfer or myself can end the tutorage if it is decided to terminate the enrollment. As long as there is progress, I will continue to offer my help. The many details involved in making such an endeavor succeed will be worked out in due time. I don't foresee older or seasoned players being invited, but there could be exceptions. Mainly, I want a place for the kids who can't afford costly lessons to learn the game. Maybe other places will open up and take care of those we won't be able to accommodate, as I think we will really have a hard time choosing which ones to invite. It will require your approval for the name, James. I will have everything spelled out in a manifesto to be finalized very soon,' Jack concluded.

'I am finding it hard to handle everything you have just announced. You just finished a record golf tournament victory, and you are retiring. The news about your new swing is really the story here, so my question pertains to Mr. Ben Hogan. Why did this not catch on in the golf community, and why was it not better known, as it has for you', Jim asked.

'Mr. Hogan developed the dreaded 'yipes' in his putting. He could not control his stroke as he had during his illustrious career, and he began missing short putts. I believe this fact kept him from using his innovative swing as he would have liked to. Also, his legs had been badly damaged in the wreck and shortened his career. I do not know why any other pro golfer never used this in his game or even mentioned it. Maybe they did, but they never spoke about it.

However, this could be the reason Mr. Hogan had so much success after the accident. Look at the wins he had, even with his balky putter. Sam Snead also suffered this way, but he did not stick to the traditional stroke as Hogan did.

CHAPTER FORTY-NINE

My next question has to do with your daughter and Tony Carpo (Smithe). Do you intend to offer to teach either or both this new technique', Mr. Carraige inquired?

'I do not foresee either Anthony or Susan using this in their golf swing. Any change in a long-used golfer's game is a hard and dangerous process. Many top-ranked players have had their careers literally destroyed by tampering with just small areas of their approach to this game. I want to teach young players only the standard and accepted techniques and let my swing changes just be mine. Maybe someday, others will spend the time I did on this method. It will not be a part of our teachings at our new school, he said.

CHAPTER FIFTY

I want to end this interview with a statement regarding my family's and my future. We hope to always be a part of the organization being put together to operate the casino and our Academy at the beautiful 'Texas Land Grant.' This place will be well guarded, as we still face the possibility of hostile action toward my family and me. I rate such danger as very low to nonexistent, as we have made great progress in demonstrations made to show how such actions would be very dangerous to those who might still hold grudges against us. We look forward to this place becoming an American tradition, Jack Proctor announced.

'FORE'-Warned
Book III

CHAPTER ONE

The sun was setting over the desert, which extended only yardsfrom where the Proctor family was lounging around their swimming pool. A ten-foot solid fence separated the property from the wasteland on the other side. Jack had acquired this land yearsago and had named the tract 'The Texas Land Grant' in honor of his father. The home and surroundings were a very small part of the large acreage that was now the site of the best casino in Nevada. This pieceof desert was outside the city limit of Las Vegas, but the new ownerenvisioned the expansion of the city in this direction.

As his dream became a reality, there was a whole lot of speculation about who owned this piece of land. The deed was registered to one of his dad's obscure corporations, with no legal connections apparent in its formation to the Proctor name. The property became very valuable, and there were many attempts to find the owner and buy the land. Jackhad plans, but none included selling.

He applied for and received alllicenses and permits to open a casino, though he never used them. He built a championship golf course around a country club and hotel with cabins along the property lines and left room for a future gambling site.All of this became a reality last year when the new casino opened as the most lavish in town.

Jack had built their home near the edge of his property, which was away from the casino and golf course. His years of living under the shadow of the mafia's contract in his life fashioned this attempt to protect his family, even though this danger no longer existed, or so he thought. He bought a large tract of desert abutting his boundary, ensuring there would be no backyard neighbors. The same instinct had led him to keep and expand the security company that had protected them all these years. The stated reason for their existence was to usethem in the casino and golf course for security. Really, this was a small part of their business. Jack could not relax his vigil when it concerned his family.

This mindset has directed his thoughts toward expanding furtherinto the desert. For several years, he has searched extensively for underground water on his property. He had formed a crew for this project. This was encouraged by learning of three pools found a few miles away. He funded an extensive survey in all the terrain betweentheir location and his holdings.

There were numerous places in the valley to the north that indicated the presence of the magical resource.He would be able to begin the small village he envisioned on the desertside of his home today, without being dependent on the Hoover dam. He could remember the good times with neighbors, a main street, schools, and a big park in his youthful home. Someday, he felt his family would need companions, all living in peace.

CHAPTER TWO

The two daughters of Jack and June Proctor had just finished their college year. The older one, Mary, had graduated, with the younger Susan having her senior year coming up. This was the first occasion when the entire family had been together for several months, and there were indeed a lot of events and plans to bediscussed. It was late in the month of May, and the weather was nice.The high temperatures would come later to this area where little rainever fell. The building of the magnificent Hoover Dam only a few milesaway made it possible for this city to be here. The Proctor family was luxuriantly enjoying the cooling waters the dam made it possible tobring to this land.

'It is so nice to finally be through with school. Everything was cool, but I am ready to begin my career in administration at the Casino, and it will be wonderful living here with you guys, Mary said.

'I'm glad you have had your plans work out for you. Mine are all messed up, especially my so-called love life,' Susan said. 'You know I broke up with Anthony. I haven't told you about his latest reaction. He has acted very badly, Dad. I hoped he would understand my feelings, but it is all about his undying love for me.'

'Mom, I have a whole bunch of years to be a woman. I thoughtI needed a man in my life, but I realize Tony is not the chosen one, at least not right now. I want to make this last year in school to be alearning period, both scholastically and athletically. I can't accomplisheither at the same time, being a woman in a relationship. Does it make sense, folks?' she said.

'Sure does, Susan. You are on the right track. However, I want tohear about Anthony's behavior, Jack said.

'Well, his feelings were hurt when I limited our intimacy to a fewhugs and kisses from the beginning. I am sure matters would have been different had I not happened to find out about his relationship with his dad. I could not get it out of my head how he swore to harm you.

However, a rough side of his nature came out big time when I told him I was not going to date him anymore. He demanded to know the reason, but he refused to consider my explanation.He stormed out of my dorm room in a huff, but he called my cell shortly thereafter. I did not answer, so he texted me an apology for his actions. This went on for two days before he visited again. I asked my roommate not to leave before I let him enter. He asked her to leave,and he became angry when I requested for her to stay. I told him to leave after he began berating us both. He only left when I started to call security. I have refused to see or talk to him since, Dad, she said.

CHAPTER THREE

Jack acted on this information immediately. He called and asked for a meeting with Mrs. Carpo, Anthony's mother. She was his partner in the newly opened casino. They had combined their assets, with Jack running the golf and country club portion. He had hired Tony as his honorary pro to connect with the professional golf tour.

'I wanted to tell you in person of my decision to terminate your son's contract with our golf business. It is both a personal and family matter, he said.

He first inquired of her whether she had been in contact with herson recently. It would have made his explanation for his action mucheasier had mother and son already discussed the couple's breakup.

'Yes, Jack, I know about your daughter's decision to stop seeing Anthony. Does this go back to the actions of his father? she said.

'I'm afraid it does, but only as an afterthought as Susan explainedher motives to me. This seems to be a case of two young people notready to make a lifetime commitment, with each having their own dreams shattered. Unfortunately, a lot of people become caught up in the consequences and form opinions unrelated to the facts, Jack said.

'Susan wants to pursue a career in golf. I have decided to be her teacher. We have agreed she must devote herself almost completely to the training regimen I have laid out. She explained to us the factht Anthony did not accept the limited role he would have to play in this scenario. An argument ensued, with some unacceptable words being spoken. Susan told us that at this moment, she recalled her feelings when she first heard about Tony's pledge to his father to harm her dad. Itseems this was the reason she called off their relationship', he said.

'We will be at the golf course every day this summer. It will takeaway from the work we need to do if Anthony is around. This is thereason I am asking him not to play here for a while. Susan will be playing in her senior year at college and will then turn pro in hopesof making the game her career for a few years, Jack said.

Mrs. Carpo was troubled by these events centered around her only remaining son, especially since it all comes from their connections to the death of her three boys many years ago. She had devoted so much of her life to separating Tony from her husband's mafia business. She knew her efforts had succeeded, except for the pledge Anthony had given his father on his deathbed. Nothing was going to make it go away and now all the mistrust was thrust front and center again in her life. Would it damage the partnership she had formed with JackProctor, she pondered?

'I hope this will not impact our business arrangements, but I suspect there may be some effect from this which will create problems we could encounter later. Please voice your concerns. We are a part of the best operations in the city. Let's try to keep everything clicking,huh', Jack said.

CHAPTER FOUR

The interest being expressed about Anthony Smith was nothing compared to the turmoil boiling in his own mind by his reactionsto the events of the last several weeks. All the emotions he thought were gone and forgotten lay fresh and exposed. Vivid memories, as real as the difference in his last name from his mother's. She had changed it to separate him from his father's mafia connections. Yet, those werenothing compared to how he was reacting to Susan's behavior and words.He could not shake the feeling that all of this was coming from her father.He could place no blame on Susan or himself. It was all because of JackProctor driving this wedge between them. He had made a promise concerning this man. A profound oath to his father he had forgottenbecause of his love for Susan. Was this the end of their love affair? Is italso the end of the reason not to act on a promise he made?

Tony felt all was lost when he got the news he had been relieved of his job as the pro-golfer at his club. He did not believe the move was made in good faith. To him, it all pointed to a concerted effort to make sure he was separated from Susan permanently.

CHAPTER FIVE

Susan was preparing to begin golf lessons with her father. Shehad found it had put the problems in her personal life out of the realm of 'life-changes' to 'lifesaving'. She realized some decisions are made 'for' as well as 'by' oneself. She recognized that her desire to excel in a sport did not diminish her life as a woman. It would beher development as a human being moving forward in her 'evolution' toward adulthood.

'We will begin our journey today in the studio I have set up witha bunch of equipment to record all phases of your golf swing. Fromall angles, to be viewed in various speeds, to let us familiarize how youdo things. We must see what we have, so changes can be made where necessary,' Jack said.

'But first, we will see from my and Ben Hogan's game what it iswe are aiming for. All our instructions will be to adapt to your stylethe lessons we have learned. Some of these will fit right in, while others will be your adaptations. We will end up with a third versionof the 'Hogan Special Golf Swing'. It will be yours, Susan. Not mine or Hogan's. We have only an idea and a dream about what it will be. Hard work and determination are necessary and will be needed fromboth of us, but the results will be yours alone, he said.

They spent the day looking at the golf swings of Hogan and her father. These were displayed on a large screen from many angles and speeds. After many repetitions and explanations, Susan began to pick up on the differences caused by the elements introduced by Mr. Hogan, especially the actions of his hands during his swing. Her Dad explained the move as a 'pronation of the wrists'. In his book, Ben described the results as producing a higher and softer landing shot.

'After the notation in his book, I could not find where Ben Hogan ever mentions this innovation again. He said the change was used about 20% of the time. I believe he introduced this variation to be used primarily at the Augusta Open. Lee Trevino stated he could not play there due to his usual shot being a low trajectory ball. Hogan's success after writing about this alteration was remarkable. However, he suffered from his putting for the rest of his career as a golfer. So did Sam Snead, but he tried many ways, some very wild, to overcome this. Ben Hogan did not, sticking to mainly orthodox systems,' Jack said.

CHAPTER SIX

For the first time he could remember, Anthony found himself at a complete 'lost' of direction for his life. It was not a pleasant situation since he felt everything was beyond his control. He realized it all started with Susan and his reaction to her decision about their relationship. When he became convinced that she was committed to her career without him, he knew the actions he took were not mature or helpful. Regret began to replace anger, and the desire to explain this to the 'love of his life' became an obsession. He decided to write her a Letter of apology.

As the young man began to weather his depressing attitude, out of the blue, two figures from his past came to call on him. No one from the many people associated with his father's past 'family' had ever approached him in any way, so this event alerted his senses. Paul and Nick had been workers in the Casino under his father. Low-ranked members he barely knew. This put him in a defensive state of mind, and the atmosphere was noted by his visitors.

The most striking feature of the men was the difference in their ages. Paul was the older, mature person. It was evident he played the role of the 'alpha male' due to both his age and physical status. They were dressed nicely, and Anthony was impressed. This fact raised his need to find out if there was more than one reason for this visit.

'We were out in this part of town, Tony, and decided to look you up. We are the last of all your father's crew left in this whole part of the country, did you know that? We loved our time as part of the 'family' and miss the old man. We heard you were fired as the golf pro and were surprised you did not join your mother working at the casino. This is what prompted our coming to see you. Nick said.

'I am sure you are aware that my mother kept me from my father's business. My brother's untimely demise made her completely convinced I should have no connection with his casino operations, so why the sudden interest in me', Tony said.

'We don't have another reason for this visit, Tony. That chapter inour lives is closed. We were approached by another Family to connect with them, but their offer was laced with comments pertaining to your dad's problems caused by the Proctor incident. We loved working withyou guys, Paul said.

'I am sure glad to hear those words, Gentlemen. No need to mention which family you are referring to. They still have a very strong desire to get a foot into this city. I'm going to ask a favor, guys. Will you let me know if New York approaches you about me or my mother', Tony said.

CHAPTER SEVEN

The summer was coming to an end, and school for Susan was nearat hand. She was happy with how her golf had progressed andrealized the hard work and time spent with her father served a dual purpose in her life. Golf remained the focus, but it helped her mind handle the emotions of her everyday life. She found out quite early that dismissing Anthony from that life was no easy matter. Maybe shewas in love with the guy. This became a positive thought after reading the letter she received from him. It struck her immediately as a heartfelteffort for him to wipe away his past reaction to their situation. She accepted his explanations but did not respond to him. Time will tellabout her feelings. Right now, she was busy moving on with the nextchapter of her life.

'This session will be our last for now. You are on the right path, Susan. I want to make one comment as a means of advice. Try not to sweat the small stuff. You are smart and talented, and everything ahead of you is learning lessons of life. Chapters in your 'Book of Life'. The Big Stuff is yet to come,' he said.

CHAPTER EIGHT

Mary noticed a subtle change in Mrs. Carpo. Their work together was smooth and refreshing, and she was learning so much about the inner workings of the business. The stress on the mother of Anthony could be observed as well as sensed. She went out of her way to be friendly and competent to show respect for the 'mother.'

She mentioned her concerns to her family. 'How are things going, Dad', she asked.

'Well, I am concerned about the future of our arrangements withthe Carpo family. There has been a development of much concern. Tony had a visit from two past members of his father's 'family'. Oursecurity people are on it, so don't mention this to anyone. We want to see where all of this goes without alarming or alerting folks.

However,we need to be very careful. This family could be in danger, so stay cool. This is the situation. We have monitors in Tony's apartment. They are not high-tech equipment. Not well hidden for a significant reason. Weare aware he knows they are there, and this is by design. He will notallow anything to occur there that is unlawful or shady. If he takes meetings elsewhere, then we can start worrying. We want him to blame the FBI.This whole mess could go in several different directions. I have a lot of faith in the young man. There is a lot of pressure coming down on him,' Jack said.

Susan had not mentioned the letter she had received from Anthony.She now spoke up, revealing his regret for the words and actions towardher. 'I agree with Dad. I am going to continue with school and golf andlet my relationship with the guy rest for this year. It may be forever inthe past. Right now, my concerns are for his mother. Can't we ease herburden somehow?' She said.

CHAPTER NINE

The casino's security people were treating this matter very seriously. They agreed to leave the FBI in the cold at this time.

Through their contacts close to the agency, it was known theywere not actively concerned about their client or anyone in this area.However, the company had information that one mafia family still had an axe to grind with the Proctor folks. All of the attention seemed to befocused in this direction. It was known the mob's leaders were not interested in going after their client. The question arose as to how far the rogue family would pursue their personal vendetta. Was the appearance of the two men at Anthony's apartment the first step in their effort to accomplish two things? Get back at this family and getback in Nevada gambling? A lot was at stake. The sudden visit by the two men once associated with Anthony's father did not appear to be a casual event. They were on the list of 'people of interest' and had beenchecked on as a regular matter. In their routine report to Mr. Proctor, this was the topic of highest priority.

CHAPTER TEN

Hardly anyone called her by her given name, which was Reba. It was Mrs. Carpo, except for her late husband. Her Italian heritage was the backbone of her life. Family and religion were the reasons she never opposed the path of life taken by her husband.It was an easy decision to continue his pet, his 'company,' as he calledtheir casino. She had worked alongside him through the years and felt the pain the infamous 'bet' inflicted on the family. Yet, she never felt the need to find fault with the actions of those people inside their organization who failed to follow procedure. All the efforts to find andpunish those responsible seemed a waste of time and effort. To go afterJack Proctor all these years seemed futile, but she knew how this actionlooked to the other families. Her feelings reflected the fact that her valuesdid not condone violence where only money was lost and that couldbe replaced. Her reaction did not match how everyone else responded. Their efforts to avenge the 'Bet' lasted a long time. Even after thedeath of her husband.

The only incident she regretted of her husband's actions was demanding their son go after Jack Proctor. Anthony had never been a part of the business due to her constant efforts. The man could havelet all the anger and frustration die with him instead of placing such a burden on their one remaining child.

Her management skills drew the praise of most of her workers andall the staff. Every one of the members of the 'family' was gone, and the casino became her operation completely. She felt shocked when Tony's scene with Susan and his dismissal at the golf course were known to her. The whole structure of the joint venture she had arranged with Jack was in danger, and she must act at once.

The call to her son's phone went unanswered but not unnoticed.The device vibrating against Anthony's chest was ignored. He did not want to talk in front of his two companions. The ring pattern alertedhim to whom the call was from. He needed to talk to her face-to-face and ease her concerns about his actions.

CHAPTER ELEVEN

Anthony sat across from the two men, talking about his late father and the love they felt for his family. They were discussing thebusiness family, not his mother or him.

'As you know, I never was a part of Dad's operation. Mom keptit away from our house. My brothers' deaths were the worst of her life. She had a motherly love for them, but protecting me became hertotal focus in life, along with running her casino. She is a strong-willed person, and I will never do anything to hurt her,' he said.

As he talked, Tony was watching his visitors closely, alert to any reaction of theirs. He knew something was the reason other than acasual chit-chat. He knew very little of them personally, so it had to beabout his father's business. He sensed from Paul's body language that he was the one to focus on.

The two men glanced at each other as Paul started to speak. Beforehe got a word out, Anthony raised his hand, brought it to his lips, andpointed to the ceiling.

'Are you guys hungry? I am. Let's get a bite,' Tony said.

CHAPTER TWELVE

They rode in silence as Anthony again gestured with his hand tobe quiet. At the small café, he asked to be seated in the rear. Afterplacing their order, he spoke.

'My apartment is bugged. It has been a long time. I found the device, took a picture of it, and had Mom's casino security look at it. They felt it was the FBI. I never told them it was in my place. Instead,I told them I found it in my father's den. I knew nothing was ever going to happen where it was, so I left it alone. I was afraid you mightsay something, Paul, is why we are here,' he said.

Again, the two men made eye contact, and Paul spoke up. 'I should have known you are a smart cookie. Man, your whole demeaner toward us has been one of caution. Well, we will be up front as to the purpose of our visit. We, too, are under surveillance due to our connections with your dad. Other than that, we are clean. We miss our old jobs and wanted to let you know we heard of what has gone down with your projob and love life. However, now there will be some wild speculationssince you have chosen to leave your pad and come here to talk. Whatdo you make of this, Tony'. He asked.

'I have cooled off since everything went wrong between Susan and me. I blamed her father, but I can see where she comes from. I wrote to her and told her of my regrets. All of this has brought pressure on my mom, because of her business deal with Mr. Proctor. Your visit will not make it any easier. If you have anyone else involved in this meeting,then I really must be careful,' Anthony said.

'Do you think we should go the casino and talk with your mother?We want to visit the place and introduce ourselves, in case she doesn't remember us, Paul stated.

'I'll tell mom who you are and for her to alert her security. I'm sure they have you on their 'watch' list. It will really get interesting when we all show up. After my actions with Susan, I know they will watch me like a hawk, he said.

CHAPTER THIRTEEN

While the three men had their meal at the café, all their actionswere being discussed by the Proctor security company back at the casino. Paul and Nike had long been under their 'radar,' so this meeting set off bells within their networks. It becamea two-alarm situation when they left the apartment. They rushed towhere they were seated but could not establish voice intercept. Afterlunch, Tony made a call on his phone to the Casino. 'I got your call,Mom. I was busy. I am on my way to see you and talk. I'll be there in an hour', he said.

'I wrote Susan, apologizing for my actions, Mom. She has not responded, but I am satisfied she will accept my feelings. I do not expect a reply, but I am really hoping to be forgiven a little. I did notanswer you because of the company I was with. Two of Dad's old crewcame for a visit. They made every effort to assure me they were notassociated with anyone. It really does not matter. I am going to assumethe worst and hope for the best. They want to pay you a visit, if it isok with you. My big concern is your situation. I will work hard to leteveryone feel at ease with me. My love for Susan hasn't changed,regardless of the future. I will not cause any more problems. I'm goingto try for qualification on the minor tour in Asia. My agent is working on it. I have called Mr. Proctor and informed him of my plans and assured him I will not be a problem to anyone but myself. Once again, I'll hope for the best. he spoke.

CHAPTER FOURTEEN

Susan was packing her 'stuff', getting ready to leave tomorrow for school, when her father came in. 'Just got a call from Tony, Susan.He is working on earning a spot on an Asian tour, he said.

She could only stare at her father. In all the scenarios as to her future with Anthony, nothing like this has occurred. Her first thought was if he could qualify. He played good golf for a country club pro,but here was a different deal, by far.

'Dad, can he make it with his game? If he can't, is there something we can do to help him? I should ask if you can help. I want him to succeed. He needs a boost right now,' she spoke.

'I have watched him practice and play. There are several areas where I could help if he ever would listen or want me to work with him. I have free time now, after all the grind you and I have been through. I will go to his mother and explain what I hope to accomplish with the guy. I can make a few calls to people who could smooth his path in a big way. I'll get on this right now, so put this item on a back burnerif you can. There is nothing you can do, so let it rest', he said.

CHAPTER FIFTEEN

Paul and Nick walked into the casino, dressed to the NINES. They drew attention from patrons and staff in a quiet way until Security alerted the floor people who they were. They did this for a couple of reasons. One, in case they gambled. Second, for any possible action out of the norm.

Mrs. Reba Carbo and Mary Proctor were on the floor and witnessedthe men's entrance. 'I know these men. I believe they worked for Mr.Carbo. I wonder what this is about', she said. At this moment, the pitboss approached with confirmation of their identity.

Paul spotted the two women, and he and Nike walked to where they were.

'It has been a while since we last saw you, Mrs. Carbo. I'm Paul Mosso, and this is Nike Conte. You may remember, we worked for your husband,' he said.

'I recalled your faces but not the names. This young lady is Mary Proctor', she said.

Their facial expressions and body language left no doubt they recognized the last name. It was also quite evident the men were impressed by both women's female attraction. This sexual appeal was apparent all around. Low-key and subtle, the men portrayed a masculine aura. Paul was the older one by a lot of years. It was morea father-son two-some, and it seemed to fit in the range for them as wasthe case with Reba and Mary.

'We have recently had lunch with Anthony, Mrs. Carbo. I hope we have convinced him we have only one reason to be here currently. We want to see the place and say 'hello'. This was our first trip back, and Tony was very nice to us. I can see from the attentionwe are getting right now that you are on full alert. Please let us know if you prefer us to go now or allow us to be a couple of 'tourists' for a few hours. Paul said.

'I agree with my son concerning your reasons for this visit. You have arrived at a very disturbing time, as Anthony has broken up with his girlfriend, who happens to be Mary's sister. His actions were notnice at all. I'm in business with the Proctor family, and such conductdid a lot of damage to our relationship. We are working hard to keep the affair away from this casino. Mary is my assistant, sent here to learn and help. Your visit creates problems for both of us. I know you realize the history behind our relations. We hope your presence has nothing to do with those past events. I am going to proceed under those assumptions. However, Security will insist we stay on alert, so enjoy our new casino, Gentlemen,' she said.

<h1 style="text-align:center">CHAPTER SIXTEEN</h1>

Jack Proctor left a message on Reba Carpo's phone that he neededto talk to her. This was not expected and was returned with a sense of discomfort. The woman was all nerves due to the events happening the past couple of days and feared more bad news was comin, her way. She felt a lift in her mood when Jack answered her call with his request to talk to Anthony. He explained it was to offerhelp to her son in his future golf plans. In fact, she was almost in tears when she thanked him. The load on her shoulders eased a whole bunchabout the future course their two families would take.

'I can help Tony in several ways, Reba, but he must tell me he wants myhelp. I will be able to improve his golf swing. There are a few places hecould use some assistance. I have already contacted some people who arewilling to offer their expertise. So, let us get busy. There is another matterwe must discuss. We are aware of your two visitors. It is not a big deal so far, but we need to be alert. Please pass on to Security if anything unusualcomes up. They check out good right now, which is fine, he said.

Anthony jumped at the chance to receive help from Jack Proctoron his golf game, but he was much more pleased to know the man held no big beef with him about his treatment of Susan. Things would never be the same, but at least there was room for hope for the future. A time was agreed upon for their practice session.

'Before we get into our work, I must address the presence of yourtwo visitors, Tony. What can you tell me about them?', he said.

'They have made a big deal of their reason to show up. I don't have any way of knowing the truth, but I feel the older Paul is more likelyto be what he says he is. He is much more at ease, and this could come from maturity. However, there are certainly separate agendas here. I'm sure Security is working full time for answers, Paul said.

'Yes, they are on it. I'll pass along your observations. They met Mary and your mother, and there seemed to be an attraction between Reba and

Paul. Also, the same attraction with Mary and Nike. Maybe thisis a good means to find out if they have other motives. I have watched your mother, Paul, and she misses her family life very much. Whenyou leave, she is going to need company in a big way. Mary and Rebaare mature women and do not need supervision, so I will observe fromafar, but with a keen eye open. Now, let's get into golf,' Jack opined.

CHAPTER SEVENTEEN

'I will not mess with your core game at this time. It is pretty good and will improve when you go up against other players. Rightnow, let us look at your grip. Besides putting, here is one place open for variation. Tony, we want to comment on your 'strong grip'.It is not really a good term. Maybe we can describe it as too strong for your swing. You either must bring the swing up or weaken the grip a little. Let's go with the latter. Much easier and better, because you havea good swing. There are small adjustments you will try out on the rangeuntil we get everything 'aligned', so to speak', Jack said.

'Next, our first task on the driving range is the same word, namely 'alignment'. I've noticed you work on several things on most swings. It is much better to have only one item on the plate at a time. Let's start with the direction of your shot, namely, alignment. Think only of this. It starts with the feet placement. There are four directions a shot cango- straight, left, right, and up. There are variations here – hook, fadeor slice, and high or low. All these elements must be considered. Learnfrom how you place your feet. We have multiple cameras to recordevery angle of the set-up. Start with efforts to hit straight shots. I finda seven iron is the best one to use when distance is not a factor. Hitnumerous balls from this one position. Try a different feet placement. Don't mix your sessions. Stick with how you started until the end. Inother words, repeat, repeat, and repeat some more. The desired result is'muscle memory.' Don't confuse practice with warm-up sessions. Theyrequire different mentalities at different times. Get into a set routine.We know there is a warm-up in every session. Sometimes, it doesn't involve your golf swing, but a group of exercises you should engage inalmost every day,' he said.

Tony admitted to himself when it all began these sessions, he would not enjoy the work. He always knew the need for practice, but his natural skills carried him along without the hours some of the other guys put in on the range. All those habits are now a thing of the past. Jack

Proctor has not only transformed the physical part of his golf game. He has changed the whole outlook of his expectations. He looked forward to their meetings. Now, it is up to his abilities and determination to become a better golf professional. He will begin his first tournament entry in five days. He could not tell Susan, as she was in school. Jack said he would pass on his desire to talk to her. 'She will be following your progress, Tony. She asked me to let you know this. Your letter was shown to everyone, and it was needed and most helpful. I know it will be difficult to put aside these other matters while on the course. I found it helpful to talk to my caddy when distractions came to mind,' he said.

CHAPTER EIGHTEEN

Eba had begun looking forward to the meetings she had with Paul as she made her way around the different games. He was usuallyat a crap table and suspended his gambling when she approached.

At first, Nike was at his side but never took time off for a visit with her.The other difference between the two men was the amount each was betting. Paul stayed for the most part at the minimum level and played a smart game. Nike was less skilled and much more aggressive. Oneman won while the other lost, heavily. All of this had occurred overseveral months, so Security was aware of the changes.

Later, she found Paul alone at the tables. Reba asked about Nike one time, but she received a vague reply and never brought it up again. Then it went from occasionally to no more Nike playing with Paul.

'Nike has decided there are more exciting people and events, Reba. I know you are looking for reasons, so I'll tell you that things have cooled between us. It is a great deal to do with his attention to Mary. I am sure you see this, and I can tell it upsets you, he said. looked at Paul with a deep stare and a solemn face. The man became very nervous under her gaze. She broke the spell, got up, and left without a word spoken. He sat without changing his positionfor a couple of minutes. The development between the two guys had to be addressed, but he could not decide on the best way to discuss it with Reba. There was another issue that must be discussed. It wasthe apparent attraction growing in their encounters. It was a slow, steady love he now felt for her. Many years had passed since his wife had died. With no children and very few family members left, he had resigned to his life alone. When Nike approached and suggested this adventure, he was ready to go.

CHAPTER NINETEEN

In the beginning, Mary enjoyed the attention from the handsome young man. There was some flirting from Nike, but Mary never envisioned a lasting relationship coming from these encounters. It was all public meetings until he asked her for a dinner date. She agreed,and Reba arranged the penthouse apartment for them. This suite was reserved for high-rollers and their parties and came with a full staff. Mary made sure these people would not leave until the date was over. The presence of waiters, busboys, and chefs throughout the evening put a complete damper on Nike's plans, and he became quite irritated with Mary as it grew apparent romance was not on her agenda.

 Mary had accepted this date eagerly, but it soon hit her that they were not in the same lane. There was an urgency in Nike for their relationship to advance to the highest level. Subtle remarks, constant attempts to touch. This was an unacceptable pace and direction for her, and she made it clear to Nike by her body language.

Reba was keeping a wary eye on the couple and picked up on what was going on. After the meal was concluded, she came through thedoor and announced Mary was needed in the office right now on a serious matter. The date was over.

Mary and Reba were absent from the floor for almost a week. The excuse that was offered was that business kept them busy in the office. It was done on purpose, mainly for Nike's benefit. Since the apparent split of thetwo men and the end to any schemes involving Mary, everyone knew his next move would reveal his true colors. He would leave at once ifthere was not an agenda. One, two, three days passed, and he continuedas before.

Paul observed the actions of Nike. He did not know the date but could read about the young man's plight through his body language.

He had failed with the girl and with him. They were waiting him out. At this moment, Reba walked on the floor and headed straight for his table. She leaned over and whispered in his ear. He arose and followed her to the special penthouse elevator, which they entered. Nike saw this action and walked toward the restrooms. Four men fell in step withhim and escorted the man down a side hallway. No one paid attention to this due to an uproar from the slot machine area. Someone had hit a big winner. A perfect scenario executed without any fanfare.

They rode in the elevator in silence. It was because Paul could not speak. As soon as the doors closed, Reba reached down and held his hand. The gesture signaled to him all was well.

Reba led him to a couch, still clutching his hand. 'We have only a few moments, Paul. Security is on the way, and they will get answers to the questions you will be asked. I must hear from your lips the whole of your and Nike's plans. Grabbing both his hands, she turnedand faced him, waiting.

'Nike came to my apartment, and after a few beers, he told me he wanted to come to Vegas to visit Anthony. He said therewere a couple of reasons. Tony was having a tough time. The other was to see the place where we spent a lot of time working. I did notbelieve him. When we left your casino, there was no communication between us, and there was not a close relationship before. I thought itwas strange he would seek me out now. However, I accepted his offer tocome here together, but only if he became clear about all his intentions.I brought up his connections to a particular mob family in New York. He finally admitted the Don of that crew gave him a special mission toget back to work for you. He never satisfied me as to what his final goalwas to be until I saw how he focused on Mary. The guy has a sordidpast involving women, and I knew he was on the prowl.

At this moment, I realized why I had been chosen to be here. I wasto attract you, Reba. Nike let the cat out of the bag when he asked me to make a move on you, he said.

'I moved to the other side of the hotel and haven't spoken to him since. I did not have to be told I had put myself in danger, so I did notleave this place, he said.

'Jack Proctor has the best security team in this country. They found out the scheme was to get you two guys into our inner circle andgo from there, wherever it led. They took Nike after we got in the elevator. Jack worried he could be a really cannon at any time, so now his sponsors know we are on to them. We let them off the hook the lasttime they moved against us. I expect there will be more actions takenthis time. I brought you up here to hear your story and find out whatto do with you, Paul, she said.

Paul moved toward Reba, his eyes never leaving her face. Stroking her hair, he pulled her into his arms. His next intention was to ask ifshe could see a future for them as a couple. It became a moot point when Eva pressed against him in the female gesture of love, passion, and surrender. He picked her up and crossed to the bed, kissing her as he walked. Their need for intimacy awakened a long- time suppressedpart of being a woman she enjoyed so much. Both soon became drainedof passion but not of the contentment of love. Paul began singing thesong – 'After the loving. It fit his mood exactly.

Reba picked up the house phone for a call downstairs to Security.She informed them everything was fine with Paul's connection to the scheme from the mob. She asked if they could delay until tomorrowany need to question him. She placed another call to Mary, telling the young lady she would see her in the morning, offering no explanation. Paul heard the conversation and knew he would have the pleasure of this lovely woman's company the rest of the night. This brought a smile to his lips and a tingle to his body. They had a lot to learn from each other in a relatively short time.

CHAPTER TWENTY-ONE

Susan looked out over the people who had gathered to see the golf play about to begin. Her scans were always to pick out her 'security gang' sent to protect her. While she spotted the regulars, there seemed to be others present, and they were busy markingeveryone in the crowd. She moved over to the water cooler where one of the old hands was standing.

'What's up, Guy. There are extras, and you all seem nervous', she said.

'Your father asked us not to alarm you. There are people on the prowl, it seems. An incident has occurred back home, so you might be in danger,' he said.

She turned and headed for the locker room and dialed her father.He explained what had happened and gave her the low-down. He assuredher all was under control and for her to go about the day. He would callher as soon as she finished. Her thoughts were mixed. Was Anthony involved? This mess kept coming back like a sore thumb. How could she concentrate on golf? Her father had reminded her it was becauseof her keen sense of awareness that made her nervous. Stay cool, was her thought.

CHAPTER TWENTY-TWO

Halfway around the world, another golfer was preparing for his own tee time. Tony would begin his tour tomorrow, but his thoughts were many long miles away. His mother had just called, informing him of the events around her. The information wasalarming as the two women most dear to him could be in danger. Rebahad stressed the fact that matters were under control, and the reason for her call stemmed from her motherly wish for his good luck. Anthonylaughed at her attempt at levity at such dire times. Right now, he hadonly one desire, which was to talk to Susan Proctor. He settled for arequest to let her know he wanted to wish her good fortune.

He had no idea how this day would proceed. All the work put into his game meant the mechanics of his swing were ready. It was the mental part where the doubt lay. Then, he recalled the advice Jack had given him. 'Put aside the little things. Stay the course. They broke up laughing when he spelled out the word 'putt.' He had developed a solid physical game and was confident he would pass the test in the long run. 'Be patient in all ways' were the thoughts that put him to sleep in this strange and distant land.

As he slept, the topic of conversation among a group of men turned to him. A few other Americans were starting this tour,as well as a larger number from Europe, but his swing and posture stood out prominently. Several of the expert golfers commented about it with high praise when this translated into a very goodgame during the practice round he played. None of them knew a thing about him until one man identified him as the past Pro of Jack Proctor's course in Vegas. Another spoke up and pondered if Tony was his protégé. Their speculations grew the next day after he posted a very good score. The media picked up on this, and word spread across the big pond. This did not sit well with the security people at the casino.

Now, their problem has become international. Susan at college. Anthony in Asia and Reba and Paul had not finished their 'meeting' in the penthouse. Then, there was Mary. This was not as serious since she was at the casino or the family home most of the time. However, she was a target to be protected. They had problems, for sure.

CHAPTER TWENTY-THREE

Jack Proctor heard some good news this morning. Susan seemed settled at school, despite the scare about the moband the worries that Tony was in trouble. It was plain to see that his little girl had boy problems. And there was this 'boy', away offon the other side of the world, doing his 'thing'. Reba had talked to her son and commented that most of the conversation focused on Susan. Otherwise, he was doing quite well over there. He was told that a British newspaper posted an article about the connection betweenthe two of them, which might be a sponsorship arrangement. Then, there was the stunning report about Reba Carpo and Paul 'whatshisname'.Jack considered that great news. If Reba found the man worthy of herlove, then a concern he had carried for a long time would be erased.Namely the lovely lady's future life. He would hear more about this since a meeting with Security and the whole gang had been set up fora luncheon confab.

CHAPTER TWENTY-FOUR

Security started the meeting with the news that the FBI had visited them yesterday. A source had reported their rogue NY familywas behind a scheme to take over our enterprise out here. They wanted to know what we knew. Nothing was our answer. Our adviceto you is to continue this narrative. We do not have any loose ends now. Reba Carbo has informed us that she and Paul want to be placed in our protective custody program. To disappear from the scene, thereby removing one danger. Nike has left the area. The family does not know anything about the two assets sent here. We questioned the man in such a way as to learn he never reported on the rift betweenhim and Paul. He was just on his way to meet face-to-face since calling was not safe from us or the FBI. He is now in a secure locale.

New York needs to establish contact, so they will send someone. We will know who they send it to. Maybe they will go after Anthony and Susan since they are the only ones off the reservation, so to speak. We will know all about it also. Well, we recommend a full assault on those people. Let the other gangs know what they are doing. Without telling too much, get the Feds involved. Take out some of their keypeople. We have been working on ways to do this for a while, and complete details are in place and ready to go. This seems to be the onlyway to kill this cancer.

The big surprise was the couple sitting close together, holding hands like teenagers. The transformation of Reba Carbo was amazing. She had always been a class act. She never let her guard down, maintaining an air of a good Don's wife. Now, her job of runninga casino brought forth her Italian character of leadership, and she was leaving to become a housewife again. It meant Mary would be the boss if she could handle the task. Jack knew Mary was to be incharge. He would make himself available to back her up 100%.

However, there was another train of thought arising in his head. He began to realize the casino and what it represented caused all this mess.

Adding to this were the mounting problems every day in running the place. Even the slot machines were beset with labor-related headaches. Although attendants were not needed, as at all the other games, maintaining them required a large crew. Every element of the casino was becoming more expensive to keep running. This part was manageable. The humans required to operate the place were reaching the phase of 'Unmanageable.' There was a different union for almost every position, but they demanded the same answers, namely more money and more control.

CHAPTER TWENTY-FIVE

For some time, I have become more perplexed with the problems of owning and operating a casino or any such business. Adding to the normal pitfalls, we have been plagued by issues that are deadly. Folks, I am to the point of quitting the gambling part of ourbusiness, Jack stated.

No one present had ever thought of this happening. To hear it from Mr. Proctor was mind-boggling, to say the least. The casino would bevery hard to close or sell without undermining everything around it.

'I have a plan. Hear me out. The gaming operations occupy only the main floor, with a few exceptions. I envision filling it with college classrooms and including the balcony area. The first couple floors in the hotel can be utilized, giving us space to attract students to a 'desert paradise'.

'Some time ago, I planned on the incorporation of all my land holdings into a village. Yesterday, I did it. By this action, we cannotbe annexed. We extend quite a few miles into the desert. Included is a large underground pool of water, a long way below the surface,the ownership of which comes with all the mineral rights I possess on the property. No one wanted this barren piece of Nevada because of lack of water. They would not allow the Hoover supply to be used sofar away. The source of my 'pond' will be sought to undermine myexclusive rights to it. We have it covered and the resources to defend those rights. The village we will establish over that spot will be ourhome, folks. Wind and solar panel farms will add to our 'OFF THEGRID' arrangement. Truck farms will complete the job,' Jack said.

'I want to expand our golf facilities around the course by adding another full-sized and minimum course. Also, a much larger driving range. I foresee Susan and maybe Anthony running a school for all golfers, big and small, young and old. The new big course would be world-class, maybe hosting a major tournament someday. Our family could become good. Let us all work toward such a goal. It would be of benefit and great value,' he said.

CHAPTER TWENTY-SIX

Jack was seated in the conference room at the casino, along with all the bosses representing the unions working in his business, including his attorney. It was a sad day for the man.

He had always had a good relationship with every one of the trades. It all began to change with a noted effort to gain more control by numerous grievances and threats of stoppages. As he scanned the group, it was evident by their looks and body language that they were ready for a war. He felt sorry for all the good workers he knew whowere about to lose their jobs.

Each union presented their demands, laced with their stories of bad experiences among the rank and file. There was a lot of cheering and applause from them. Jack could not keep back a smile at the superiorair of victory emulating from the group.

Jack rose to speak. They were not prepared for what he announced.Not a word about any of their demands. No mention of his expected surrender. Only the short, curt announcement that the casino was going out of business as of the next morning. All activities will close at noon tomorrow. He advised that the meeting was over and ordered them to leavethe premises immediately.

CHAPTER TWENTY-SEVEN

Jack sent a notice to all the unions, along with a release to the media. He had mailed this to the proper authorities the day before, to be received today. The reaction was swift and brutal from the unions, populace, and the State. He had included an additional letter to the unions, in which he expressed the lack of warning, and each person would receive a severance check. He knew the gaming folks would demand some type of meeting, so he decided that would be the opportunity to reveal his plans for the building. Because it was within the newly incorporated 'village,' no outside rezoning would be required. Planning could begin right now.

'I figure the rehab of the building and the construction of thegolf facilities will take about one year. Susan will graduate around then, and Tony should be ready to come back to the States. We willspend that time working on our oasis out in the desert, making it into our 'Garden of Eden'! We should be through taking care ofour problem pertaining to the threat from New York. Our security folks had asked to be released from our exclusive arrangements. They had been approached by two of the big boys on the strip to provide similar services as we have. I'm working on selling my interest for future considerations we will need later. Everything is pointing to anew 'beginning' next year. I expect each of us can make the decision on our own future before then. I am hoping we will all be together. With the business of gambling come many dangers. We have been the target largely because of the greed associated with it. I pray thiswill end for the betterment of us all. Our new endeavors will bring much pride and joy, I hope, he said.

CHAPTER TWENTY-EIGHT

Susan found out early in the year that her career was not goingto be centered on golf. It would remain a large part but not the driving force. She slowly began to realize that being a woman was not just a physical happening. It was the power behind her being. This came from her maturity in mind and body. It was nice to be able to play the game her father loved so much. Yet, it did not fill her needs, especially at night before sleep won out over her thoughts. She missed Tony more each night. Holding hands. They talk to each other.She decided to write to him as soon as she first sat down at her desk.

He answered with news about his tour. Mostly, they were newsy notesbetween friends. Susan filled him in on all the happenings at home. Tony replied that his mother had told him about Paul and Nike. As the weeks went by, their notes became more personal, and they both knew there was a future for them if it was handled in the right way. Anthony kept everything low-key as they moved along in their separate worlds together. This arrangement was exactly what they both needed. Time to mature in each their own way and time. Susan thanked her father for having faith in Tony. His work with him gave the man in the boy the chance to have a purpose.

They really enjoyed playing golf. It had been a long time since they did it together. There was at least one day each week when they experienced the pleasure. Tony knew he was the cause of their friendly matches coming to a halt. They were separated by many miles and different agendas at the present time. They were too close for too long a period before. Tony had expectations that did not match Susan'sbut insisted on having his desires fulfilled. He was fortunate to have this second chance. The time we are apart right now will tell us about our future together.

CHAPTER TWENTY-NINE

The closure of the casino sent shock waves throughout the state, as well as the city. The only good news coming from the event was that it was not caused by a lack of clients or gaming activity.

The bad news was a reason given pertaining to the labor force and the activist unions. Every gambling business in town suffered more each day from unhappy employees. Action at the games was steady and strong throughout the strip, so profits should be higher. This was not the case. Another reason was that more and more politicians had their hands out, demanding illegal kickbacks. A large percentage of the ownerships were large corporations able to absorb these extra costs by passing some to their clientele. Higher prices for food and hotel rooms were the order of the day.

The action of Mr. Proctor got the attention of a certain mob family in New York. They had sent two men to the city on a mission which had to remain a secret. All the other members of the New York group had ordered a hands-off on this casino. These two are now missing. Suspicions were mounting that the two events could be connected. The same family was let off easily the last time they went after Jack Proctor, and they got caught. A couple of new people were sent to find the answers. Wait and see, was to be the order of the day. Meanwhile, work had begun on transforming the casino into a shd

'We must complete this project, so there is no doubt we are out of the gambling business. Most of our problems have been associated with the casino. Now, I feel is the time to kill two birds with one stone. Let it die and raise our new adventure from the ashes, so to speak. Susan and Tony are doing great. The media has picked on their careers by connecting them to our family. They are suggestions; we are creating a dynasty of sorts. I propose we name our new venture 'Proctor Sports Academy'. We want to attract sport-minded families to our facilities while focusing on golf. We want to go forward while erasing all traces of our past gaming life, he said.

CHAPTER THIRTY

The paths of Susan and Anthony were moving closer together, day by day. Right now, they were a long distance apart as the crow flies but growing together in many ways. Tony had carried a big load on his back because of his parents. For so long, he was cast in a role he could not handle, and he ran away from it. Susan became the direction of all his hopes, which almost became his downfall. Now, his mother had found her new life, and all was well in that respect. Susan and her family had given him a second chance. He was a happy person after years of uncertainty. He could not foresee the collective outcome of his new confidence, Susan's career, and the "Proctor Sports Academy". Jack could, and it all was centered around and a part of their 'Texas Land Grant' estate.

The end of Susan's college career was getting close. The final tournament was due next week, and she has been established as one of the favorites. Her father laughed at the final seeds. One school had pushed heavily for their entry and had influenced the directors to put her on top. 'You can't have politics in sports.' This is such a blatant move and threatens the whole day. A trans male in a college women's golf tournament. I do not blame Susan for withdrawing,' he said.

Protests were deemed to be acts of terrorism, and the tournament went forward, even though four schools pulled out. Susan announced she would no longer play in any form of official golf events. She was going home to her family abode and join their business.

Anthony was dismayed when he heard of Susan's plight. The last event on their tour was due next week, and he had been viewed as the favored golfer. However, the directors made it clear that they were not opposed to the direction pro golf was headed. He withdrew, packed his bags, and headed home to Susan, his mother, and the Texas Land Grant.'

CHAPTER THIRTY-ONE

Security has extracted the full story from Nike, and it all starts with the same New York family we had problems with in the past. The Don has not learned his lesson. I have asked them to contact each of the remaining families and give them a choice. Take care of the matter themselves, or we turn it over to the feds. We have proof they are engaged in activities that are still going onto this day. Action must begin now,' Jack said.

Meanwhile, back at the new 'Big House' in the village, there was a huge reunion taking place. Susan had arrived and was greeted by her parents and sister. Standing at the back was Anthony, his mother, and Paul. They celebrated for the first time as a new family. Jack was impressed by the warm and loving way they hugged and kissed each other. Yet, that was nothing like the excitement generated when Susan approached the group. She walked straight to Tony, giving him a bear hug. It was a moment no one present expected to ever happen only ashort time ago.

CHAPTER THIRTY-TWO

All work had been completed on the transformation of the casino to "JACK PROCTOR ACADEMY". The first class will enroll shortly. The professional in charge of golf for the men will be Anthony Smith. For the women, it will be Susan Proctor Smith. The president will be Mary Proctor. The CEO will be Reba Carpo. Jack Proctor will remain in the background, available for support. He has done his good work and turned everything over to the next generation.

Time marches on!!

THE END